JOHNNY'S WORLD

The Series-In-One

JOHNNY'S WORLD

The Series-In-One

John W. Sangwin

Copyright © 2025 by John W. Sangwin

CITIOFBOOKS, INC.
3736 Eubank NE Suite A1
Albuquerque, NM 87111-3579
www.citiofbooks.com
Hotline: 1 (877) 389-2759
Fax: 1 (505) 930-7244

Ordering Information:
Quantity sales. Special discounts are available on quantity purchases by corporations, associations, and others. For details, contact the publisher at the address above.

Printed in the United States of America.

ISBN-13:   Softcover   979-8-89391-849-6
                eBook   979-8-89391-850-2

Library of Congress Control Number: 2025916195

TABLE OF CONTENTS

Part one: JOHNNY'S WORLD… The Beginning

Part two: JOHNNY'S WORLD… The Early Days

Part three: JOHNNY'S WORLD... Life Goes On

DEDICATION PAGE

I would like to dedicate this book to my wife, Patricia Ann Tisdale Sangwin. She has endured my writing the earlier five books that made this one possible. I also want to thank various friends who have prayed for me and encouraged me with supportive words. I also praise my Lord and Savior Jesus Christ for allowing me the inspiration and words to place on these pages.

FOREWORD

Let me speak to you for a moment as the actual author of "Johnny's World. "My writing approach for this book may be considered unusual by some, but for someone like Earl Hamner for instance it would be quite recognizable. First of all, I am not the character Johnny Sampson. The name indeed came from my childhood. My mom particularly referred to me as Johnny prior to my second birthday. Our neighbor, Mr. Taylor, called me that name often. The character Tinsley Nathaniel has Mr. Taylor's first name. So, you can say that I might be a blend of both. The fictional writer, Nate Thomas, is the grown-up version of Tinsley Nathaniel. Nate has the benefit of being able to look back and know what we call our "fictional future." Sure, some character's names have surfaced from somewhere in my past but not necessarily as I knew them. The title character is Johnny Christopher Sampson. His first name is as explained, while his middle name comes from the fact that he is a "Christ-like figure and Sampson is a strong figure in the Bible. There are a few other names used which readers may notice and wonder if they were an influence. Let's just borrow a phrase from a popular T.V. show, Dragnet. "The names have been changed to protect the innocent." I can just hear the title theme song!.

Book Introduction

My name is Nate Thomas. When I was a child, our family moved down south to the small town of Appleton into what I have learned to call "Johnny's World." Life was difficult back then, but we learned how to truly live a life, not just exist. Many names have become life-long friends. Johnny Sampson, Bruce Lightfoot. Walter Davidson, Carol Benjamin and others whom you are about to meet. Hang on as we visit what I have affectionately called *Johnny's World.*

BOOK DESCRIPTION:

This book explores the influence one child has in helping another child become accepted in a world that isn't always friendly. It is a family book. It will relate, stimulate, and create memories that even the mind can't hide.

Part one: JOHNNY'S WORLD… *The Beginning*

CHAPTER 1

A NEW START

As a young boy of six, having a tough life wasn't all that tough. Sure, I was getting uprooted and being forced to go to a "foreign" territory to live.

My given name at birth was *Tinsley Nathaniel Thomas*. To my dad, I was Nathaniel. To mom, I was Tinsley. Eventually, I settled with just plain *Nate*. Our big move happened because dad got laid off from his job. He had been with the same company for five years and it had paid well. Dad had just received an offer to work as a plant manager for a manufacturing plant that processed apples and transformed them into other products. My favorite was applesauce. The hardest thing to understand was that there were apples growing in the south in a town called Appleton, U.S.A. Mom was a schoolteacher in a Christian School. Since it was summer, she could freely look for a teaching job.

Here we were, on the road trying to reach our new home. Mom had told dad, "Nathan, how can you possibly find a job that paid as much as what you were making?" Dad answered, "Alice, we'll just have to leave it in our Lord's hands. He will provide as long as we remain faithful to Him."

Moving day was longer and not what this kid had expected. We were on the road for what seemed forever and didn't even reach our new hometown. Dad had suggested, "I think it would help both our minds and bodies if we stop and have a good meal along with some rest in a nice soft bed and as for you Alice, you can get a soak in a nice warm bath and what you call "beauty sleep". Dad chuckled as he said that which got him a poke in the ribs.

No one had asked me for my opinion about moving. They probably figured, "Oh, Tinsley is just a kid, so he'll do what we say." At least supper was good, and I enjoyed a great big banana split with a cherry right on top!

That next morning, along with the roosters (and yes, I heard one), we were back on the road again! As we drove into Appleton, I thought, "I sure could use a tall glass of apple juice from that new job of Dad's." He had located a house not far from his new job and close enough to the school I would be attending, so I could either walk or ride my bike. It appeared to be a nice quiet neighborhood.

As I look back on what I know now… we were destined to become an important part of what we would call *Johnny's World*. Our house was located just two doors away from the Sampson family. Between us was a older gentleman who lost his wife a few years earlier. It was midday when we pulled up in front of our new house.

I noticed a group of children playing across the street just down from our house. Mom suggested, "Tinsley, why don't you go down there and make friendly with those children." I'd never really had any friends, so why should I begin now? Remember, you are Tinsley Nathaniel Thomas, I thought to myself. That thought didn't help much and all I knew was that I wanted to be me, whoever that was.

While the movers worked alongside my parents, I took a walk down the sidewalk in the direction of those children, but on the other side of the street. Suddenly, the door of the house I was passing flew open and out came a boy bouncing on a polo stick. "Look out!" he yelled, and before I knew it, we were in a heap on the ground. The kids across the street came running, hollering "Johnny, Johnny, are you all right?

"Hey," I said. "I think I'm O.K." I picked up my large-framed glasses and brushed myself off.

One of the boys looked at me and said with a glare, "Okay four-eyes, why not watch where you are going!" The boy I ran into was getting up. He brushed himself off and immediately extended his hand to me. "Are you okay? I'm Johnny Sampson.

As soon as I let my name out of my mouth, those other kids burst out laughing. "Hey Tinsley, were you born in a smarty-pants hospital or something?"

With my head hung low, I turned to go back to the mover's truck and what happened next will stay etched into my mind forever. Johnny said, "Hey Tinman? Could you use some help unloading?"

After stuttering for a moment, I said, "Sure." Over the next several hours, I began to get to know more about the boy Johnny in *my* "Johnny's World."

CHAPTER 2
A BUMPY BEGINNING

The next few days were busy ones. As a family, we had lots to do to get our house in shape to live in. I had my own room again, and Dad painted it just as I wanted. It became a "Sky" blue with "Eggshell" white trim. Everything else in the room was shades of brown. Yes, everything: rugs, lampshades, blinds, bedding, furniture, picture frames- you name it. Everything!

The day I got my room in order; I invited Johnny and his friend Bruce Lightfoot over to see it. I especially wanted to share with them my *scientific encyclopedia* set.

Neither of them seemed very impressed, although Johnny did ask several questions, which kept the conversation going. All Bruce did was stand around smiling with his hands in his pants pockets.

As I sit here writing down my thoughts and experiences, I fear I may leave out something of great importance or something that would be better to present a clear picture of my life growing up in *Johnny's World.*

Just before I turned six years old, my dad, Nathan Allen Thomas, and my mom, Alice Marie Tinsley Thomas, had the greatest idea ever. Mom brought home a brochure from the Christian School she worked at. Her being a teacher benefited me during my preschool days. She was forever looking for ways to add to my already advanced way of thinking. Even before home-schooling was popular, she was getting me ready for that wonderful experience called "*school.*"

What mom did was that she talked dad into ordering a complete set of those Encyclopedias for only $129.95. Included in that price was a complete index and full colored maps and a bonus book of science facts. Dad had told her, "You know Alice, that I haven't ever said "no" where our boy's education is concerned.

Those next few weeks, while I waited with much anticipation, I drove my parents near insanity. They loved seeing me excited, but my asking, "Are they here yet?" was almost too much. One day, Mom replied, "Tinsley, so help me, if you don't stop asking day in and day out, you may become a scientific experiment!"

The day finally arrived when the deliveryman brought my special delivery packages. I had just got home from school and as soon as I heard the knock at the door, I ran as fast as the road runner himself.

"Mom," I yelled, "My scientific encyclopedias are here!"

Mom answered, "Now, Tinsley, how do you even know what the delivery is? Perhaps it's something your father ordered or one of my teaching aids!" Before she could finish that statement, I had the first box opened and was looking through one of the books.

From that point in time and throughout that first summer, I spent most of my waking hours reading, researching and just plain absorbing all that I could. I kept getting stuck in areas pertaining to science. My young imaginative mind began to open. That subject included works by Edgar Allen Poe, Jules Verne, H.G. Wells. While other kids may have been playing in the streets and allies, I spent time traveling all over the world, in my mind.

One day, Dad had gone to get the mail and was in his study for quite some time. When he came out, he was unusually quiet until all of a sudden, he announced, "I have decided that since I have accumulated lots of time at work, it is time I take off and take the family to Washington, D.C. and tour the Smithsonian Institute."

Dad suggested that I get information from my encyclopedias and make a few calls around and plan out the details for our "vacation." Our itinerary included a stop at the National Museum of Natural History. While there we learned of scientific things dealing with Nature, particularly a live beetle collection. That same day, we went to the National Museum of History and Technology. Many exhibits concerning our country's growth in science, the arts, and technology.

While we were checking out the cotton gin, I had to ask Mom what I thought was a legitimate question. "Mother, when you and dad got me that sweater last Christmas, was it made here or somewhere else?" Dad quickly replied, "Tinsley, why on earth would you ask that?" With a tone of confusion, I responded with, "Dad, well the label on my sweater said '100% Genuine Cotton/ Made in the U.S.A." Mom immediately gave me a look that told me to think first before putting my foot in my mouth of which I very well knew how to accomplish.

The next day, we spent time at the National Air and Space Museum. There we saw the Albert Einstein Spacearium and got to see the Wright Brother's display featuring the Kitty Hawk plane. While in the area, we saw the Capital, Jefferson Memorial, then rode by the White House and the Washington Monument. I thought I waved at the president, but he did not wave back.

Our last day was spent at the National Zoological Park/ Washington Zoo. We will always be thankful for our Aunt Dorothea who made it possible for us to have such a memorable trip. When we returned home, dad had to tell us the news about his job which led the way to our planning our move.

My encyclopedias probably never meant as much to anyone more than me. For years to come, I used them as much as people today use Google and their trusty phone.

The day after showing my new friends those books, Johnny said, "Hey, Tin Man, let me introduce you to our other friends. You've met Bruce. This is Walter Davidson and Carol Benjamin. On their bikes are Walter's siblings Diane and Ken Davidson."

Suddenly, a high-pitched voice yelled from Johnny's house. "Johnny, mom wants you!" It was Johnny's sister, Ann. "I'll be there in a minute!" "I'll be back as soon as I can" Johnny told me. "Go ahead and get to know each other better."

All I really wanted to do was go home. After a couple of minutes had passed, Diane Davidson asked, "Tinsley, run into anyone lately?" The whole group laughed. I just stood there with my hands in my pants pockets.

About that time, I heard my mom calling me to come home. Very quietly, I said "See you all later." Later that same day, Johnny came by and asked, "Why did you leave so soon?"

I shrugged and said, "Mom called me home, and besides, I don't think anyone likes me." Johnny's reply was, "Give them time, they'll come around."

Later that evening, Dad informed us that he would be starting the new job the next workday and mom had an interview with the schools as well. Change was coming, and my world would never be the same.

CHAPTER 3

TIN MAN, LET'S GO FISHING!

Dad did indeed begin his new job, and Mom had her job interview. In a couple of weeks, she would begin having workdays to prepare for school to begin. She was so excited! She reminded me that I needed to make friends. After all, Johnny had told me that his sister, Ann, had already read ten books this summer! So, when Mom said, "You could go to the library and do some early studying before school begins. You'll want to keep your grades up," it made sense!

As I went out the door, it slammed behind me. I cringed as I knew I would hear mom yell, "Tinsley, don't slam the door!" I had planned on riding my bike while exploring the neighborhood. Down past our block was a corner store called Dorman's Quick Stop. I wondered just how quick the stop could be?

I decided to head down the next intersecting street which was named Orchard.

Down on the right was a house painted with almost every color imaginable. I wondered who lived there. One day, I hoped to find out. In the next block was a fire station with a big number 5 by the door. The fire trucks were so shiny and clean looking. Did they ever use them?

While heading home, I noticed Johnny, Bruce and Walter going toward my house. Without thinking about it, I honked my new horn that I installed on my bike. It was loud and very high-pitched. The guys stopped and Walter yelled, "Man, where did you get a horn like that one? It could wake up my dead relatives!"

Johnny just shook his head and said, "Hey, Tin Man, you want to go fishing?"

It took me a moment to realize that someone had invited me to go fishing with them! To answer the question, I shrugged and replied, "Uh, I've never been fishing."

Bruce muttered, "He probably doesn't even have a pole," "That's all right," said Johnny. "I have an extra."

We hurried on to my house so I could let mom know where I was going. The next few hours were very interesting. I lost several worms before I caught a fish (Johnny had to handle the worms).

My first-ever catch put up quite a fight! (It wasn't even a foot long!) By the time we were done, Johnny had six good-sized fish, Bruce had four, Walter had three, and I had only one. Johnny suggested we put them in our cooler and "if our parents agree, we could plan a fish fry sometime soon."

I felt disappointed and rather embarrassed about my one fish, but Johnny said, "Don't let that bother you. After all, Jesus fed more than four thousand people with just a few fish."

"Really?" I said, "You believe that story?"

"Of course, I do," said Johnny. "It's in the Bible, and the Bible is God's word!"

Snapping back, I said, "So you're saying my one fish 'could' feed more people than I could imagine?"

Johnny replied, "Well, I'm not Jesus, but with God anything is possible!"

So, in a couple of days, our families got together along with us fishermen. It was a wonderful time, and I think my fish really did multiply!

CHAPTER 4

RAINING ON A SATURDAY

As I think back on what it was like being that child, Tinsley Nathaniel, there weren't many worries. Each day was a new day. Fresh and exciting. I recall one of those first Saturdays after we moved to Appleton. We had planned a family outing to a nearby park: Johnny's family, the Sampsons; Bruce's family, the Lightfoots; and our family, the Thomases.

I began my morning with what I thought was early for a Saturday (it was 8:15 a.m.). Mom and Dad had been up for a while. They had breakfast and had prepared our contribution of food for our picnic. I quickly began to get ready for a fun day with my friends and family with great excitement. I had set out what I wanted to wear the night before, which included a new pair of sneakers (they were black and white with the whitest laces you've ever seen).

Suddenly, I panicked. Shouting out loud, I said, "Mom, where are my eyeglasses? I can't find them!"

"Have you looked on your nightstand?" she replied.

"Oh, I didn't see them." I reluctantly answered.

"Why not try opening your eyes and looking a bit before getting all worked up!" she said.

"Mom, I guess I am a little nervous about getting together again with our new friends. The fish fry was so much fun that I'm just overly excited!"

There's nothing like fun in the sun on a Saturday and that's when my life, as I knew it, began to end- so I thought. I heard a loud noise outside that sounded like thunder. Quickly, I ran to the living room and looked out a window. Dark, blue-green looking clouds were in the distance, coming from what I knew to be the northwest. We were about to experience bad weather, southern style.

Not today, I thought. "Mom, Dad… please, don't tell me it's going to rain!" Dad responded, "Son, I won't tell you that, but I've been told that this region is known for some rather intense storms that come through in the summer months and that's only a prequel to Hurricane season."

"Dad, that's the same as telling me!" Quickly, I ran out the door and ran down the street to Johnny's house.

Knocking as hard as I could, I heard a voice that I knew was Mrs. Sampson saying, "One moment! I'm coming." The door opened and there stood Mrs. Sampson. She was wearing an apron.

As I stood there, raindrops slowly began to fall. Without thinking, I said, "It's going to rain."

She stared at me and said, "Yes, I believe so!" At that, she yelled, "Johnny, Tinsley is here!"

Johnny came running to the door and said, "Tin Man, you're early!" I wondered if he had even noticed the weather.

"Johnny, it's going to storm and ruin our Saturday!"

At that comment, Johnny smiled and said, "Oh, it will pass, and the sun will be out in a couple of hours."

I acted as if I fully understood the weather patterns of the South. "Johnny, don't you see those dark, blue-green clouds? That can't be good." The wind was beginning to pick up, and the rain had gotten harder. "Johnny, what about our picnic?"

"Tin Man, it isn't even 10:00 a.m. yet. Besides, God will take care of it. There may even be a rainbow for us to enjoy!"

As he spoke, I could hear the tap-tap sounds of hail hitting the roof. Mrs. Sampson said, "Tinsley, you might as well wait here for the rains to move on through. I'm sure your parents are concerned about your safety with the sudden change in our weather."

"But what about our picnic?" I replied. That simply was all I concerned myself with. I gazed out the window, and all I saw was darkness and gloom.

Once again, in a calm voice, Johnny said, "Tin Man, it will be O.K. Give it thirty minutes, and we might see some sun by then."

Suddenly, I remembered a time when Mom told me, "We must put our faith in God and wait on Him." I figured that this must be one of those times.

Sure enough, thirty or so minutes later, there was that sun, and my, what joy I felt.

In spite of my doom-and-gloom attitude, in His time, God came through and even sent that rainbow! As I look back, I can say, "Johnny, you were right again!" All was right in Johnny's World.

Later that same day, after our picnic, my mom received an invitation for us to attend church the next morning. I thought to myself, *I wonder what this new day will bring.*

CHAPTER 5
CHURCH ON A SUNDAY

Back when we were living in the east, we attended a large Independent Baptist Church. It was difficult getting to know everyone very well. Our Sunday School classes were big which allowed us to have many activities. Even our children's choir program was big.

Now that we live in a small town, I expected to attend a much smaller church and we do, but only in size. Johnny's family belonged to The First Central Baptist Church of Appleton. The people and ability to minister was bigger than any large church on the east coast. As soon as we walked through the front doors we were welcomed with open arms. The Sunday School Director, Bro. Carl Jones, greeted us and brought us to our classes.

When I walked into my "class" or Department, I saw Johnny, Ann, Bruce, Walter, Diane and Ken. More than thirty children were in that room. A lady up front was making announcements. She was Mrs. Pam Johnson, the pastor's wife and Children's Director.

Johnny motioned to me that he had saved me a seat, so I gladly sat down. I could feel every eye, I thought, on me. Very soon, we broke into classes by grades. Our class teachers were a married couple, James and Caroline Martin.

As I reflect on what we as a group of young learners were about to hear taught on that first day in that church which had quite a history of its own. The pastor at that time was the Reverand Jimmy Johnson, but as we trace back through time, we learn some very interesting things.

The first homesteaders that founded Appleton settled in an apple grove near Apple Creek in 1868. The creek got its name from all the apple groves that seemed to spring up out of nowhere between 1861 and 1868. The talk was that soldiers during the Civil War were responsible, by spitting apple seeds all along the creek banks in areas they made camp.

In 1871, a group of Baptist families who had settled north of town on the western bank of the creek, decided to form what would become the First Baptist Church of Appleton.

In 1872, another group did the same thing toward the south, but on the eastern bank of the creek. That church was named the Central Baptist Church of Appleton because it appeared that most of the town's population was living there.

Eventually, the town spread out toward the south, causing many people to move south. In 1945, Appleton had lost many of its young men due to World War II. Change was necessary. After seventy-four years of ministry, the First Baptist Church merged with the Central Baptist Church and became the First Central Baptist Church of Appleton. By 1955, the church outgrew that location, and a new facility was built in the next block. By the time we arrived in Appleton, the church was large for a small town but smaller than our big-city church back east.

Yes, the present-day Pastor, Reverend Jimmy Jack Johnson was the third pastor since the merger. He was married to Pamela Katherine Stewart. They never had children, although they have claimed all their church children as "family."

The lesson for that day was about Jonah and how God had instructed him to go to a town full of people he didn't know. He was to go show a bunch of strangers that God loved them by example.

Jonah was afraid so he told God, "No!" God didn't like that answer so He sent a big whale-like fish to eat him. Jonah wasn't hurt, but what a tummy ache that fish had. (That brought a thought to me as when we would ever get to go fishing again.)

Lucky for Jonah, he changed his mind and went just where God wanted and preached the message God gave him. It was a message of love to people who needed to hear it. When class ended, we headed to where the preaching service would be. Music was playing, and a man got up to lead the choir.

We sang some songs, one of which I knew. It was the one that says, "Jesus, Jesus, Jesus, sweetest name I know… keeps me singing as I go!"

Shortly afterward, the pastor, Reverand Jimmy Johnson got up preached about friendship and how Jesus "could be our best friend, if we let him!" His His words left me thinking.

One thing I realized was just how much of a friend Johnny was becoming. He didn't have to show me kindness, but he did. As we prepared to leave the church, we all held hands and sang, "Oh, how I love Jesus! Because He first loved me."

Me? Yes, even me!

CHAPTER 6
NO GIRLS ALLOWED

In my lifetime, there always has been a time when a female has a major role in life. As life in "Johnny's World" progressed, our group of *close* friends became known as the *gang*. I recall the first time that subject was put to the test. A fifth "member" of our gang received a test, of which us boys actually had to pass it. Being a girl, Carol Louise Benjamin began to come to terms with the reality that she was on the outside of our group, looking in. We guys often chose not to include her. It wasn't literal, but we just didn't *think* to include her of which we thought she understood.

The four of us "men" decided to build a fort. It was to be strong and massive. Johnny asked me (the brain) to design it. I spent a very long time (a whole hour) working on it before showing my design to my fellow builders.

In the early stage of planning, Ann, Carol, and Diane insisted that they be included. They told us that "behind every great plan there should be a woman." All of us guys couldn't help but laugh at that comment. Johnny decided that since Carol was one of our best friends, "why don't you be our secretary? You can record all of our important decisions that us "men" make and share it with you girls, so you'll know of our progress." Carol's response was "Johnny Sampson, if you think you can get me to forget that I am as important as you, forget it! I may be a girl, but I will not settle on taking notes for you guys. You're on your own!"

Carol was Johnny's across-the-street friend. Even though she was our age and was considered a good friend, she usually stayed home and read a book. She was one of those people that if she wasn't holding something to read, you wanted to ask her where it was. In school, she excelled in English. She was an excellent writer when it came to essays. She was the one to call if you needed help since she had a vivid imagination.

That afternoon, we figured it was time to move forward with the building of the fort. It would be located in a wooded area behind Bruce Lightfoot's house. Walter announced, "Guys, I got a great idea. Since Bruce is part Indian, we can appoint him to be our scout, medicine man and even…" It only took one quick look from Bruce and Walter stopped talking. "No way! In some ways you can use my heritage, but I've had enough with those kinds of comments."

Walter replied with a huge smile, "Come on, Bruce, you can be our good Indian, and we could even make one of my sisters be your squaw!"

At that comment, Johnny spoke up and said, "Enough of that kind of talk, and besides, this is our fort and as we agreed, no girls allowed!"

The work on the fort took three days. We had to borrow hammers from our dads. We searched through our neighbor's trash piles and found scrap lumber, some of which still had nails. (It's not easy to make a bent nail straight!)

The guys were so impressed with my design, especially the slanted roof and the shielded window. Of course, the window had no glass in it, but it did look great. The shielded part was simply a 2x4 nailed above it. Johnny suggested, "Let's plan an open house and invite our friends & family!" The only problem was that they would have to stay outside and look at it, unless we gave a one- at-a-time tour.

When the day came for our open house, the girls along with Walters older sister Debra came. Debra immediately explained, "Boys, I represent the girls and announce a public protest about not allowing girls in your fort." After that statement, they sat down in the doorway. Now we really had a problem!

Walter immediately exclaimed, "Hey, that's not fair! We can't even get in our fort without walking on or stepping over you girls."

The next thing we knew, a TV crew showed up to cover the so-called story. "News at ten," said the reporter. They interviewed Johnny, who shared our reason for our fort and about our "rules." They also interviewed Debra since she was their appointed spokesperson. She shared all the girl's concerns. The next day was Sunday, so we postponed any further dealings on the subject.

Our pastor's sermon the next day was very interesting. It was about avoiding those things that may appear evil and always putting the needs of others ahead of our own. He even shared *the golden rule* from the Bible that says, "Do unto others as you would have them do unto you." Oh, my goodness, what else?

The "men" called a meeting and met at Johnny's house. After much discussion, we decided to consider the words our pastor had said, so we called in the girls. "Debra and all you other girls, we have decided to use 'our' fort on Mondays, Wednesdays, and Friday's, and you girls may use it on Tuesday's, Thursdays and Saturdays," announced Johnny.

Immediately, the girls let out a "Yeah!" and began to make all kinds of noise. When they were done celebrating, Debra cleared her throat and said, "Carol has informed me that the girls have agreed to say a big thank-you, but no thanks! We just wanted to get your attention and get you to think about what you were doing. Thanks to Reverend Jimmy's message, you all have come to your senses! Please go ahead and enjoy your fort."

From that day on, we had a very hard time enjoying our fort like we thought we would. One thing we certainly learned was that you mustn't underestimate a girl.

CHAPTER 7

TINSLEY, YOU'RE TOO SMART!

All my life, I had people tell me, "Tinsley, you're smart!" I just can't help if I'm the type of person who doesn't have to try very hard at understanding and remembering most things, especially facts and figures. I have always loved science, and even nature itself is quite fascinating. My desire to read wasn't very strong, but I have managed to recall what I do read or hear quite easily.

One day, about two weeks before school was to begin, I was working on an experiment that I read about. The boys had dropped by and wanted to go fishing. "Hey, Tin Man, why don't you put aside what you're doing and come fishing with us?"

My response was one of surprise, "I'm sorry y'all, but I am in the middle of an experiment and can't just drop it. Why don't you all come back later and let me know how the fishing went?"

As they headed out, I gathered all my materials and equipment I needed and went outside to set up. Much of the information I needed was in encyclopedias. While I was working, I noticed our neighbor in his front yard. Johnny had told me his name was Mr. Howell. I told Johnny, "That sounds like something a pack of wolves would do at the moon!" We both laughed at that idea. It looked like a great opportunity to meet him since I hadn't found the time to do so.

Very slowly, I made my way over and asked, "Mr. Howell? Hi, I'm Tinsley Nathaniel Thomas, your neighbor!"

As if looking right through me, he responded, "That is quite obvious, young man. Nevertheless, I'm glad to finally meet you."

"Have you lived here very long, Sir?' I asked.

Mr. Howell cleared his throat and spoke. "Most of my life. My wife of fifty years and I raised our children in this house. We had to bury two of them. One of them died serving our country, and one of our daughters was killed in a car accident a few years ago."

"Oh, I'm sorry, Mr. Howell," I replied.

We continued with some small talk about his life; then our discussion turned toward his church attendance. "My wife & I were good friends with another couple who live on Appleton Court. We attended church together. You might have noticed the house that is painted every color of the rainbow!"

Excited to learn about the people in that house, I said, "Yes, Sir! I did notice it one day when I was riding my bike while doing a little exploring. What are their names?"

He replied, "Kenneth and Annie Miller. They raised five children in that house and have eight grandchildren and two great-grandchildren. Most of them visit every summer. You all probably just missed their visit!"

He continued to explain, "Those kids are the reason that house is painted with so many colors. One summer, they asked them to help paint the house, so they picked out their favorite color. Each kid had a different color! The Millers didn't seem to mind letting them paint it that way!" We laughed at the thought of it.

Mr. Howell and I must have talked for nearly an hour. It's a shame we as young folk don't realize the importance of reminiscing. That is the "art" of remembering.

Children do not usually reminisce, grown-up children do. Yes, there is such a thing as "grown-up" children. Those are the ones who stay young at heart. They are the ones who manage to cherish memories of childhood. Mr. Howell and I were doing just that, remembering things that were of importance, but time took them away like sand on a beach that was here today and gone tomorrow.

Memories of friends hanging out "just because". Celebrating accomplishments. Silly times. Things you did but never thought would be. Memories bring laughter and tears. They even wish you could undo an event.

I had lost track of time and forgot about my experiment. "I need to get in," he said, "and prepare my lunch. I so enjoyed our visit, young man. We need to do it again sometime."

As I returned to my project, I said to myself, 'You know, Tinsley… you're just a kid, but it's nice to act grown up and learn some new stuff and that I did today! Hey, self? You're hungry!'

I quickly picked up my things and went inside to fix a peanut butter and honey sandwich. "Tinsley, you're too smart, but not too smart to know when to give in to what is most important!"

As I reflect or remember, even today while I write these words, I recall words that were written long ago. They were recorded in The Bible. In Philippians 4:8 (adapted from NIV). "Hold on to what is true, whatever is noble, whatever is just, things that are pure, whatever is lovely, whatever is admirable, - if anything be praiseworthy- *reminisce* on those things."

So, what makes a memory? It is not a "what", it is a "who" and that who is me and YOU!

CHAPTER 8

THE FIRE

A couple of days had passed since my conversation with Mr. Howell. It was a cloudy morning. There was stillness in the air, although I could hear neighborhood children playing to get as much outside fun before school began again. I told Mom that I was going to ride my bike. I headed down to the end of the block past Walter's house and turned by Dorman's Quick Stop.

As I continued down the street, I could see Walter and Ken headed back in the direction I had just come. As I passed them, we waved and as I came nearer to the Miller's house, I could see Johnny running across the street in what appeared to be quite a rush. I was about to yell at him to get his attention, when I heard what sounded like a scream. I could see Mrs. Miller through her upstairs window. It appeared that she was trying to open it. As soon as it opened, I saw smoke pouring out of the house. Her screams of "Help!" got louder as she cried, "Please help us; the house is on fire!"

All I could think to do was honk my horn repeatedly and yell, "*Fire!*" I got off my bike and raced to the Miller's burning house.

Johnny had heard my horn and saw me running toward the house. He was on his way immediately. Walter and Ken heard my signal so headed back in our direction. I noticed the next-door neighbor as he came outside to see what the commotion was. I said, "Please call the fire department!"

Johnny went to the front door right behind me. "Tin Man, move!" Immediately, he began kicking the door until it opened.

"Johnny, it's the Millers, and Mrs. Miller is upstairs!" Black smoke was pouring out the door. The fire appeared to be coming from the kitchen.

As we entered the kitchen, we saw a frying pan with a burner that had been left on with bacon grease. Bacon grease burns easily and will catch fire. Normally, baking soda can be used to put out a small fire, but this was spreading too quickly. Also, if I had access to salt that might work, but there wasn't time.

The fire was already moving up the walls toward the upstairs, right below where Mrs. Miller was. The smoke I saw upstairs was most likely coming from the air vents. Johnny quickly said, "Tinsley, go find Mr. Miller, and hurry! I'll go upstairs to get Mrs. Miller. The fire is spreading fast."

Mr. Miller, overcome by smoke, was in the living room sitting in a chair.

I quickly managed to pick up a straight-legged chair and used it to break a window in that room. It immediately allowed smoke to escape. Walter came in and said, "The fire trucks were pulling up outside." I told him, "Walter, grab Mr. Miller's legs and help me as I get him by his arms."

As the firemen were coming up the sidewalk, we were struggling to get him out of the house. We told them, "Our friend Johnny went upstairs to find Mrs. Miller."

They replied, "You all need to get out of the house, *now*! This fire is spreading quickly!" The firemen had hooked up their hose out front and down the street to a fireplug that was yellow with a green top.

Suddenly, I heard what sounded like a small explosion coming from the kitchen. The fire apparently was beginning to spread to the second floor. "Johnny!" we all yelled. Where was he? Was he okay? Did he find Mrs. Miller?

From outside, we watched as the smoke poured out the front door. Suddenly, two figures carrying another came out. They were a fireman, Johnny and Mrs. Miller. An ambulance was waiting. The attendants began treating Mrs. Miller. She was coughing uncontrollably. Johnny was coughing some as well. Mr. Miller was already in the ambulance. They were both taken to the hospital. Fortunately, the hospital was less than five minutes away.

It took the firemen quite a while to put out the fire. It had spread to the upstairs bedroom. With both fire damage and smoke damage, it affected at least half of the house. The kitchen was destroyed. Before the fire was under control, I even prayed for one of those summer storms. "Lord, let it rain!" It didn't, but I felt so much better for hoping.

With all the excitement, I hadn't noticed the crowd that gathered. My mom and Johnny's mom were in the crowd, and I saw both the Davidsons and the Lightfoots. Bruce came running up to Johnny, asking, "Are you guys all right?"

"Yes, but the Miller's house is a mess, and oh my, all the pretty colors are ruined."

We could hear more sirens, so we wondered if another fire was near, until two cars pulled up. One was a police car and the other was identified as the Fire Marshal. The men in those cars had lots of questions, mostly directed to us three children. A TV crew arrived as well. Without thinking, Walter said, "Wow! Are we going to be famous?"

At first, I thought maybe so until things took a turn for the worse. Those next couple of days were like a bad dream. Johnny's World was about to shake, and only one word described it: TROUBLE.

CHAPTER 9
TROUBLE IN THE WORLD

The next few hours were busy ones. The questions were nonstop. All we really cared about at that time was just how the Millers were doing. No one could tell us anything other than that Mrs. Miller had been admitted to the hospital. Mr. Miller was treated and released to go home. All of us couldn't help but think *Oh my, how could he possibly stay in that house with the mess it was and not knowing the condition his wife was in?*

Both the fire marshal and the police chief questioned each of us separately. After a while, the only one they wanted to question was Johnny. Both his parents looked very concerned. I asked my dad, "What could they possibly want from Johnny?" They even asked his parents to take him to the police station for further questions.

The next day, the talk around the neighborhood was that Johnny was the main suspect for setting the fire. I found out that Mr. Worthington, who lives across the street from Walter, was the city prosecutor. So, he would be the one who could find Johnny guilty and send him to jail. His brother was the police chief. The Worthington's had two children, Billy and Sue, with whom we had dealings with before.

The Worthington children were younger than all my friends. They seemed to be troublemakers. For some reason they never seemed to want to get along with anyone. They would ride their bikes up and down the street as fast as possible and then put on the brakes suddenly, skidding to a stop. They would then say, "What are y'all looking at? Take a picture; it will last longer."

They both tried to break into our fort several times and were caught trying to listen in on our meetings. Eventually, we discovered that they were the ones spreading the word that Johnny started the fire!

The evening after the fire, I went to the corner store. I overheard two men saying, "I understand that the Sampson boy must have been stalking the Millers, because he was seen on several occasions either hanging around or running from their house."

"Yeah, the fire inspectors said there was a second fire-start location in the kitchen." I knew in my heart that there was no way Johnny had anything to do with setting that fire, other than helping to rescue the Millers.

The only thing that held up the investigation was Mrs. Miller's inability to speak. The doctors had ordered her to remain in bed and to undergo breathing treatments. Mr. Miller had been back at the house trying to clean up some. There was talk going around that it looked like Johnny might have to go to a juvenile detention center because he was underage for regular jail.

I told Mom, "This is a huge mistake. There has to be an explanation." Johnny insisted there was, but he "couldn't discuss it right now." Discuss what? Either he was or wasn't guilty.

The next morning, all of us guys decided to get together at the fort to discuss the situation. Johnny was unable to come. They had recommended that he remain home. We invited the girls to meet with us. We all had a sudden desire to pray. Walter closed our prayers and Bruce said, "We must do as our Sunday School teacher has told us when we face trouble and don't know how to handle things. Always pray and ask God to fix things and especially to bring back our friend Johnny to us!"

What a sight it was. All eight of us bowed and prayed, the best we knew how. Without further discussion, we finished and went home. Later that evening, just before dark, I heard noises out front and a big knock at the door.

It was Ann and Bruce. "Mrs. Miller is awake. She says that Johnny didn't begin that fire. After the fire on the stove started, she tried to remove the pan with flaming bacon grease in order to dump it out the kitchen door. She spilled it, causing what had appeared to be a second start for the fire. She then began to tell us, "Johnny had been helping me with early morning chores for quite a while. When he was done, he always hurried home since his mother hadn't told him he could spend time with me. I really feel bad that I got him in trouble!"

Once again, we found ourselves quite busy, but in a good way. Johnny was back with us, and we all decided to go help Mr. Miller with the cleanup. Honestly, I believe most of our church came out to help.

That Sunday, our church was abuzz. We all had a great deal to be thankful for. God heard our prayers. Yes, others were praying, but as for us kids, we knew for sure that God answered our prayers!

CHAPTER 10

WHOSE WORLD?

Thinking back on the events of that first summer in Appleton makes me smile. I met new people, many of whom I am still close friends with today. I gained confidence in who I was, which greatly prepared me for the Nate Thomas of today.

That week after the Miller fire brought together people of all walks of life, ages, and beliefs. They came to help an elderly couple who had lost a lot. Their lives were suddenly changed and through a community of concerns, so were we. Our church organized teams to work on repairing the house and aided in finishing the cleanup.

Our pastor contacted the Miller's children and assured them that their parents were indeed being taken care of. It was not necessary for them to rush back to assist.

After talking with Mr. and Mrs. Miller, Johnny had suggested that all of us neighborhood kids get together and repaint the damaged parts of the house. We could each pick from the original colors and attempt to match what we remembered. Mrs. Miller rejoiced as she said, "You children have become so important to us that we trust your "better" judgement." At that statement, Walter let out a grunt that we all understood.

The city council and mayor of our town declared a special day to celebrate the bravery and determination shown on the day of the fire. Johnny, Walter, and I were given citations and keys to the city (although I doubted, they could fit any actual doors.)

The Worthington children had to attend a meeting with our parents so they could apologize for spreading false information (and I'm quite sure I know where they got that information).

The Sunday before school began was filled with crazy emotions. I was happy we had moved to Appleton. I was pleased to be a part of a church where even the children were appreciated. I had friends, genuine friends. My parents both appeared to have jobs that they could grow in and would find peace from knowing that fact. I had another school year coming, which I was certain would be filled with adventure and that meant *fun*.

This neighborhood that I refer to as "Johnny's World" had begun with uncertainty but has taken on a transformation to be known as *…our world*.

Life without the unexpected oops is simply boring. Remember that a frown is really an upside-down smile. All you need is a little hilarity to brighten up a possible gloomy situation.

It didn't take long for us the residents of "Johnny's World" to witness various pranks that led to hilarity. If not careful, it can become mischief. One such incident was when Walter released a harmless grass snake in church that gave poor Mrs. Lulu Little a terrible fright. The incident did create hilarity, but the timing could have been better.

Reverend Jimmy had just greeted everyone with a "good morning" and then came a lulu of a scream. What happened afterwards we never talk about much. Several boys and their parents were called, and visits were made. No one person confessed, but we knew.

Another example where things aren't always seen as intended was when the pastor was preaching on the wedding feast and the Lord wanted to know why there wasn't any wine. The story was really serious and delivered from the heart until our dear friend Walter decided that he had to confess out loud to all who were present that he was guilty. "I confess, it was just a harmless prank. I put beets in those buckets, thus turning the water blood red."

As with many who confess, he then decided to run and hide, making the situation funnier and more so when Rev. Jimmy said, "Well, they say confession is good for the soul."

A story not told until now involves our friend Carol Benjamin. One summer, Carol had been complaining to us all, especially Walter, that she believed that she could out fish us boys if she only had a chance. One day, Johnny Sampson announced, "I suggest that we give Carol her chance she wants!" Walter didn't think it was a good idea. "Girls belong home and not out doing guy things" That got Walter another bop on the head. We then voted to allow her to go fishing with us on a chosen date.

That day began with Carol leading the way out to the lake. Before we got there, summer rain had drenched us all. She wasn't happy about that and told us all. She said, "I am serious about this, and you just wait and see!"

As we arrived and began to set up. Walter's bird of prey showed up which he told her in detail about. In a concerned voice, she said "Walter, you guys need to tell that thing to go away. I cannot fish with that thing flapping its wings up there! Besides, it might grab my prize-winning fish before I get it pulled in."

Walter's response was not helpful. "Carol, if I have to fish with it flapping around, so do you!" At that comment, she moved away from where she had prepared to fish next to Walter clear down to the other side of everyone. Now she had no choice but to place the worm on the hook herself. The sight alone was worth many pictures. Next came the casting of the line. "I am quite serious about this, and I will succeed!" After nearly decapitating a couple of friends, she managed to cast the line a few hundred feet. With that done, a look of victory came over her face. As she stood there waiting, there came that first tug on the line and then the second tug and yet another. She then began to panic.

"What do I do…" Before anyone could come to her aid, she slipped, landing on her bottom in mud and seeing her "borrowed" fishing pole flying like the most perfect javelin ever thrown. Without much said, laughter was immediate, and Carol looked like anything other than victorious. Poor Carol. Even though it was funny, she looked so sad that the hilarity did not last long. Everyone came to her rescue. We did our best to encourage her so as not to be completely discouraged. Walter convinced her to join him and together they caught three fish- one was quite a beauty.

Carol never asked to go with the "guys" again and we never forgot the look on her face as her pole went up, up and away!

One thing for certain, "Johnny's World" was ours and we made the best of every minute of it.

Part two: JOHNNY'S WORLD… The Early Days

CHAPTER 11
THE ADVENTURE CONTINUES

Life for me as a child was often like a *Huckleberry Finn* adventure. Johnny was Tom Sawyer, and I was becoming Huck Finn. The rest of our circle of friends, at least in my eyes, were the "gang" Tom wanted to assemble. The only difference was that we weren't robbers.

I recall that first year of school after moving to Appleton. On day one, I remember learning that my mom, the teacher, known as Mrs. Thomas—had her classroom across the hall and a couple of doors down from my classroom. My teacher's name was Miss Chapel. She was very pretty, a fact that none of the boys missed or failed to discuss. In those days, the word *chatter* meant just that.

We had heard that this was Miss Chapel's second year teaching. I thought she looked a lot like Nurse Chapel from *Star Trek*. That just happened to be one of my favorite shows on T.V. I would hurry home almost every day so I could watch the next episode. It was almost as important as brushing my teeth every morning. Because of my love for science, I could relate to that show. Nurse Chapel's first name was Christine, while our Miss Chapel was Montreal. I always thought that was a city in Canada.

One morning, as I approached the front of the school, I heard a voice, "Hey, Tin- Man, did you see our principal, Mr. Farmer? He was walking with Miss Chapel, and they looked rather friendly together, don't you think?"

I knew without a doubt whose voice that was. It was Johnny Sampson. I thought those words seemed strange coming from him until I realized he was trying to get me "upset", after our earlier conversation concerning Miss Chapel.

My response was, "I'm sure he was just being a gentleman."

As we entered the building, the first bell rang. We hurried to our classroom. I could see my mom down the hall as she was closing her door with one of those looks that you never care to see. Oh my, how just one look is all it takes to get a point across!

As I quickly took my seat, my desk nearly tipped over. I took out my pen and paper just as Miss Chapel was writing our daily assignments on the chalkboard. "Now class…" Before another word was spoken, there was one of those screechy sounds that only chalk can make. The whole class squirmed. One of those assignments included the word science, which sent all sorts of exciting sensations up my spine.

The school day passed quickly as we listened and watched our teacher walk back and forth at the head of the class. The bell announced the end of another day. As I got up to leave, Johnny and his good friend, Bruce Lightfoot, were just ahead when suddenly they stopped to turn around as if to tell me something which caused a collision of everyone behind them. As we all got up laughing, Mr. Farmer was just down the hall and very quickly approached to put an end to our hilarity. "Boys and girls, what is going on? You appear to have caused an unsafe incident to take place. I want you three boys to march right down to my office. Mr. Thomas, (as I gestured toward myself) your mother will be contacted immediately."

Later that evening, Mom admitted that she thought Mr. Farmer had gone a little far with his reaction, but he was indeed the principal. "Tinsley Nathaniel, I'm afraid that Johnny Sampson may be turning into a bad influence. He had seemed like such a nice, polite young man, until after the fire at the Miller's."

My reaction to that statement was with shock and amazement. "Mother, Johnny hasn't done anything wrong. He would never lead me anywhere or into anything that I shouldn't be involved in." The only thing I was mistaken about was how friends possess the power to control each other.

As weeks went by, school would become a bit boring. We desperately needed some excitement. One day, our friend Walter Davidson, Johnny's "never-boring" next-door neighbor, hurried over to Johnny's with a flyer he had received.

Excitedly, he said, "Hey, guys, look! A fair with amusement rides and such is coming to town. They claim to have one of the fastest roller coasters. See, that's what it says here in this flyer!"

So, in the next few days, plans were made for all of us kids, even the girls, to go to the Coleman Brother's Traveling Amusements and Arcade. They had gotten permission to set up at our county fairgrounds. Our community would definitely be excited about this event. They would be around for at least two weekends. Chances were that this would lead right into our citywide fall festival.

The only thing that could possibly dampen our hopes and plans would be the weather. As usual, I just had to ask, "Hey Johnny, what if it rains?" So, like the ticking of a clock, the day for fun had come and … what was that, Thunder?

CHAPTER 12

LIFE IS LIKE A ROLLER COASTER!

Given the events of the past summer, I should have been better prepared as the school year began. Storms come and go. As an adult, I have seen my share. Yes, even I, Nate Thomas, admit I have had to deal with disappointments as well as exciting moments in my life.

So, on that Saturday morning before going to the fairgrounds, the sound of thunder once again was as if the world was collapsing before me. Thunder brought lightning and more thunder. The heavens opened, and the rain came tumbling down and down and down.

To young Tinsley, Noah's flood had returned. If you had been there, you would have heard, "Mom, please say, 'Tinsley, it will be alright. The rain will stop just as quick as it began, and you kids will get to go to the fairgrounds as planned!'" That wasn't what came to pass. For the next two hours, all we heard was thunder and the loud pitter-patter of rain hitting our house. As I gazed out the living room window, I tried to count raindrops. I failed!

It was only yesterday that we had discussed our detailed plans for going together to the fairgrounds. Johnny had said, "Tin-Man, I will get Bruce and Walter and ride our bikes down to the end of the block, and at 8:30 a.m. sharp, you meet us there." I certainly hope the guys weren't down there waiting for me. What a silly thought! It just didn't seem right to get your hopes up one minute, and then all of the sudden you're down counting raindrops. Oh my, that's just like a roller coaster.

"Mom," I yelled, "when will the rain end?"

"Tinsley, you know good and well that it will stop when the good Lord decides we had enough!"

Just before 11:00 a.m., the sun was peeping out, and there was hardly a sprinkle.

The blackbirds were everywhere, as if they knew it was time to take flight and head to the fairgrounds. A knock at the door sent me flying to get it. As I opened it, there stood Johnny, Bruce, Walter, Carol Benjamin, and even Walter's twin siblings, Diane and Ken. "My goodness," I said. Does it take all of you to get me?'

Quickly, Walter responded with, "Tinsley, you mustn't think so highly of yourself so as to think that would be the reason we're here. We have been waiting so long that we truly are in a hurry to get to the fairgrounds! Okay, Let's go!"

So off went our merry gang of children. If we had only known what this world would be like today, thunder wouldn't have had the effect it had. Disappointment is truly in the eyes of the beholder. An exciting adventure was what we were looking for. As we approached the fairgrounds, we could smell the mixed aromas of hot dogs, popcorn, cotton candy, and all sorts of wonderful things. We could hear sounds of music coming from the carousel and, of course, screams of excitement from the roller coaster. Almost immediately, the girls began to express concern. "That sounds scary!", said Diane.

The boy's reaction was the opposite. Walter quickly responded with, "You girls are a bunch of pansies. That roller coaster ain't nothin'. It's just a bunch of fun waiting to happen."

Diane quickly fired back at Walter, "You do remember the time you wet your pants on a similar ride?"

As Walter turned all shades of red, he replied, "You know, I could tell stories on you too. I was a lot younger then, and besides, I had just drunk a tall lemonade before going on it!"

After that exchange of sibling jabbing, Johnny said, "Let's just have some fun!"

Our time at the fairgrounds was both exciting and tiring. Johnny's sister, Ann came out and joined us, as well as Walter's other sister, Debra.

As we headed home, we reflected on all the fun we had, and we were so glad the rain had stopped and that none of us had gotten sick or wet our pants. The only negative thing was that the fun was ending.

It's kind of funny to think back on that day, because little did, we know how many similar times were to follow. Smiles would come, and memories were being made.

CHAPTER 13

REMEMBERING

(What's in a Memory?)

I often ask myself, *what is a memory, and what makes it memorable?* To a child, it's usually tied directly to happiness or even sadness. Children don't usually reminisce, but grown-up children do. Yes, there is such a thing! Many adults stay young at heart. They are the ones who manage to cherish memories of childhood.

Having friends, to me, Tinsley Nathaniel, meant a lot. When we lived on the East Coast, I spent most of my free time cooped up indoors, either reading or watching T.V. Even then, I never missed *Star Trek.* Friends? Not really. My classmates back then always made fun of me for being somewhat smarter than most. The only time they warmed up to me was if they needed help with science.

Before coming to Appleton, going outside to play wasn't really the safest thing to do. You never knew who would be hanging around or what they wanted. Living in Appleton was like a breath of fresh air. I had freedom to be me. I never really had the chance to discover who I was until I stepped into Johnny's World.

One day, we were all just hanging around outdoors. We had a fire going, a controlled fire, and Johnny was watching it. All of us had gathered together, even Walter's older sister, Debra. We had been living in Appleton for a few years by now and were very well accustomed to everyone's families and each personality.

I recall many times like this where we talked of fun times and times when we shocked each other with our accomplishments. A memory can make you laugh or cry. It can even make you wish you could redo an experience. Memories of past decisions belong to those who lived them and no one else.

As we sat around that fire, we gazed at each other and remembered those feelings of friendship that only we could have. It was happiness, fulfillment and life as the Bible describes. "Hold on to what is true, whatever is noble, whatever is just, things that are pure, whatever is lovely, whatever is admirable, - if anything be praiseworthy- *reminisce* on those things" --- Philippians 4:8 (adapted from NIV).

Johnny had developed quite an interest in fire prevention ever since the Miller fire. He had entered projects in the science fair. Yes, even I was surprised. He had actually won one of them just before our year to enter junior high school.

Johnny's sister Ann was quite a homebody. She didn't seem to have much of a desire to play outside or go on adventures with the rest of us. One thing we noticed was a change in her when she began hanging around Dorman's Quick Stop about the time, she had begun junior high all because of a boy named Bruce Mayfield.

Bruce Lightfoot had been Johnny's best friend forever it seemed. He was part Cherokee Indian. Johnny had nicknamed him Fish-man. He became really interested in people's rights and how to protect those rights, especially that of fellow Native Americans.

Walter Edward Davidson was Johnny's next-door neighbor and our favorite friend to pick fun with. Usually, it came quite naturally. He was very good-natured about everything and learned a lot about life and how to get along with others from our adventures. Even today, he is sharing those experiences and has helped many other "Walters."

Debra Elaine Davidson was Walter's older sister, who was often looked at by most of us as a know-it-all who had no business butting into our affairs. In reality, she was a kind and helpful girl who was willing to help when our problems became more than we could handle. She was the first of us to get a job that eventually paid off in a BIG way.

Diane Elizabeth Davidson, Walter's younger sister, became quite a popular girl in spite of him. She was elected homecoming queen and ended up dating (and marrying) the high school's most popular athlete and quarterback. Little did we know she would end up being the most settled down of us all.

Ken'eth Edgar Davidson, Walter's younger brother and twin to Diane, really became the one to surprise us all. The only thing I'll share for now is this. I suppose you would remember troublemaker Sue Worthington. Yep, love was to be in the air for those two. Odds are that he had to take her to the shed a few times, so to speak.

Carol Louise Benjamin was what some called the "outside of the family" friend who lived across the street from Johnny. We never really considered her as such. She was the same age as most of us guys, but she was a girl. Until she turned twelve or so, she was "one of the guys" in our eyes. What changed was when we had an incident with our building our fort. We had decided that it would be best to exclude girls, thus separating her from us. She was a big reader. She and a book were never apart. She was developing quite an imaginative mind. As she got older, she kept a diary. She even entered contests involving creative essays. One point of interest was that she did indeed marry "one of the guys."

Yes, as I gazed across that campfire at all my friends, I could see how each of them was helping me become who I am today. I could only hope that our friendships would continue. I owed Johnny Sampson a lot for including me in his circle of friends. My eternal friendship was certain as far as I was concerned.

As I continued to gaze, my concentration was suddenly broken by Walter. He hopped up, and out of a bag came a guitar. He said, "Surprise! Let's sing!"

So that evening and others like it ended with us singing around the campfire. Memories being remembered and made. Bruce Lightfoot's backyard, not far from the wonderful fort we designed ourselves. Yes, memories filled with happiness.

CHAPTER 14

TIN-MAN, WE HAVE TO CATCH A *BIG* ONE!

Growing up in what I often refer to as "Johnny's World", meant that we would respond with a fishing pole in hand and ready to head to a favorite fishing spot. On a Saturday, several weeks into a school year, we would find the time to answer the call. His voice would say, "Tin-Man, we have to catch a big one". I would never grow tired of hearing that voice of him saying those words.

As the boys of Johnny's World rode their bikes to the county park to walk that half mile to the lake, the sun was shining, and the birds were singing. As I think back on that day and others like it, I can still see Johnny leading the way, his good friend Bruce by his side with our friend Walter right behind and beside him was me, Tinsley Nathaniel. Of course, he hardly ever called me by name. It usually would be Tin-Man. Often, Walter's younger brother Ken would follow muttering something about his twin sister Diane, who wasn't even there.

On the day in question, I recall it being a cool crisp Saturday morning and since it had rained earlier, there were puddles of water on the trail leading to the lake. Each puddle looked as if you could drink from it until someone stepped in it. If someone missed a puddle, the next person usually found it. Often, I would wear my favorite white sneakers. As I often heard, Mom would say, "Tinsley, you knew better than to wear those shoes fishing!" Knowing better always seemed to come too late to do me any good.

As we neared the lake, you could hear a loud, screechy sound somewhere in that blue sky. I recognized it as a hawk or some other bird of prey. Immediately,

Walter stopped in his tracks and said, "I sure hope that bird gets satisfied with whatever he kills before he makes us his next meal." Bruce, being part Indian, replied, "Walter, you have nothing to fear. As soon as that bird smells your scent, he will fly the other way!"

That comment left Walter scrambling for words. With nothing better to say, he responded with, "I suppose if it did try to get one of us, you could shoot him with a bow and arrow, right?"

"Walter, I guarantee that if I had a bow and arrow, I would be able, but I wouldn't.

That bird is no threat to any of us!" All of us just laughed, including Walter with hesitation, while we continued our walk to the lake.

When we arrived, the water was so still that it appeared as if you were gazing into a mirror at your reflection. It was that calm, until the bird of prey decided to swoop down and grab a carefree, unsuspecting fish from out of those quiet waters.

"My goodness," exclaimed Walter, as we witnessed such an amazing thing. "Better him than me," he said, as we all agreed.

The fishing that day was pretty good. I was beginning to get the hang of it. I had even talked my dad into getting my own fishing pole. The only thing that didn't change was my reluctance to handle my own worms. You might think that a science guy like me wouldn't mind it, since I could dissect a frog with no problem. Of course, they were drugged and couldn't squirm around.

As we fished, we spent the time telling stories or just plain chatting about our daily school activities. I thought, here we are on a Saturday hanging out with friends and we are talking about one of the things we hoped to get away from. Among those topics of discussion was a recent Sunday School lesson about Jesus and His disciples going fishing.

Johnny said, "The day was getting late, and they hadn't had much luck catching anything, so it was suggested that they quit. They were net fishing. Jesus told them to cast the net again but on the other side of the boat. Out of respect, they agreed." Walter then said, "Yeah, they were so successful that their nets were breaking. You know, I bet if that big bird had been there, he wouldn't have been too happy that they weren't sharing!"

Bruce could hardly wait to say, "Walter, you just can't seem to leave that bird out of our conversation."

At that comment, Ken quickly pointed behind Walter and said, "Look out, it's the bird of prey!" Walter landed on the ground facedown quicker than we had seen him move. Everyone laughed again, except Walter.

The walk back to our bikes always seemed longer than when we arrived, probably because of all the fish we caught, or perhaps because it was like work to get them home. Funny, but even on days when we weren't so successful, it felt the same.

That very next day at church, we were all amazed at our Sunday School lesson. It was another fishing lesson with Jesus and His disciples. Talking about timing, although to Walter's shock, there was no mention of a bird of prey.

CHAPTER 15

THE PASTOR GETS SERIOUS

At the time of our move to Appleton, the pastor of the First Central Baptist Church was Reverend Jimmy J. Johnson. He and his wife Pam were at our church for nearly ten years. You get to know a person rather well in that amount of time. That meant that he got to know the young people who grew up in his congregation. Since his wife was the children's director, he had plenty of inside information. While at our church, they served together as youth sponsors for our youth group. As you can see, Reverend Jimmy KNEW us well. Our "gang" fit right in the middle of both categories during their ministry.

I recall one Sunday morning during the morning worship service, when someone "accidentally" released a harmless grass snake. No one supposedly knew who was responsible. It didn't really matter according to Mrs. Lulu Little. She claimed that she might never get her girdle straight again after such a incident. The scream that lady made would have brought Lazarus plumb out of the grave, even without the voice of our Lord.

Fortunately, Brother J.J. was able to make use of the event. "Fellow members and Mrs. Little, that *harmless ..., little* snake brings to mind when Moses lifted up the serpent. That just happens to compare with our Lord Jesus being lifted upon that cruel cross for our sins!" What a reach, but it worked. Later, the pastor gave credit to us kids.

There were many times when our dear friend Walter became an example or a part of an illustration. Pastor Jimmy would get preaching, when suddenly, he would get some kind of revelation and start sharing a thought that seemed unrelated to his topic, and it almost always had Walter in it. One time, his subject was about Jesus turning water into wine, found in John 2. "And then Jesus ordered the men to fill the water pots with water." I had noticed Walter acting rather odd, as if something was bothering him. Brother Jimmy then said, "Jesus instructed those in charge at the wedding to draw some of the water out and taste it."

All of a sudden, Walter jumped out of his seat and yelled, "I confess! I put beets in that water bucket. It was me! It was me!" Walter continued yelling his confession as he ran out of the auditorium. The whole church was breaking out in laughter.

Our Pastor just shook his head and said, "Well, confession is good for the soul."

During one of our youth meetings, Mrs. Pam and Brother Jimmy were teaching us from the passage in John 3. Mrs. Pam began, "A man named Nicodemus had come seeking Jesus at night so he couldn't easily be seen, for he was a learned and respected leader of the Jews." As the lesson moved forward, the pastor looked at Walter and nodded his head. Walter spoke up clearly, "Most certainly, I say to you, unless one is born of water and the spirit, he cannot enter the kingdom of God." Later on, he reminded everyone about Moses having lifted the serpent, while wearing a great big smile on his face.

Probably one of the hardest things for a pastor is to preach a sermon at the funeral of someone you hardly knew. During our Pastor Jimmy's ministry, our neighbor Mr. Howell may have attended our church on a holiday, such as Christmas or Easter. He had told me that it was hard to go after his wife had died and even harder after his daughter died in a car accident. He said it wasn't because no one cared. "They certainly did", he told me. "and they even brought food. The previous pastor had made a visit after his wife died. Pastor Jimmy had come by a few times, but "I just didn't feel like socializing or hearing much about God's love."

That day we spoke in his front yard was the beginning of a relationship that lasted until the day he died. I remember the conversation from his hospital bed, when he told me, "Tinsley, you have been the closest thing to a real son, and I thank you for it!" His daughter would come by occasionally, and the other daughter's husband would bring the grandchildren from time to time. On the day Mr. Howell died, I was with him as well as Pastor Jimmy. I was a teen by then. In a very feeble voice, he asked me to pray for him and for his family, who were in route to the hospital. It appeared that they wouldn't quite make it before his passing. I did my best as I fought away the tears.

"Dear Heavenly Father, I come before you, asking that you bring comfort and assurance to my friend. Help him as he awaits his time…" After clearing my throat, I said "Amen." A moment went by, and he breathed his last breath. At that very time his daughter entered the room and kissed his forehead. Our pastor gave me a hug, and we left them.

Yes, the day of Mr. Howell's funeral was hard for us all. Mr. and Mrs. Miller were there. Mr. Miller was using a walker, and Mrs. Miller was in a wheelchair. Our gang of friends were there, as well as many others from our neighborhood. Mr. Howell had asked if I would read the obituary and say a few "kind" words. He chuckled a bit and said, "only if you feel like it, of course." I shared Psalm 23 and told of how he had always referred to me as someone who was "like a son", but he had actually become a grandfather I never had. Both sets of my grandparents died when I was really young. I finished by mentioning how we shared moments that were special and had even gone to his house as a family and enjoyed what he could manage.

So here we were, paying respects to an elderly gentleman who had departed this life. Pastor Jimmy, I'm sure, had prayed about what to say, but I for one never expected to hear what he shared that day. The passage he shared was 1 John 2: 28-29 and 3:1-3. The subject was clearly on our roles as children of God. He said, "We all must practice righteousness. In this world, many people like Mr. Howell live a very lonely life and if they don't see true religion demonstrated in someone, they may never be exposed to real Christianity." He then went on to explain more of the scripture and concluded with these words: "We need to examine our hearts and look at the example of a child. Our very own Tinsley Nathaniel Thomas became a true friend, while still a child to Mr. Howell. Just as Christ is pure, our hearts must become, because of the hope we have in Jesus."

Pastor Jimmy and Mrs. Pam were with us as Pastor a couple more years before the Lord moved them to another field of service. I for one, will never forget the days our pastor got serious.

CHAPTER 16

...BUT JOHNNY, SHE'S A GIRL!

In all my rambling about our so-called "gang", it may appear to you that as friends and acquaintances come and go, the same may be to it. You would be correct, because a couple of weeks before I would turn thirteen, a certain girl caught my attention. It was a beautiful spring day, and she had the brightest smile ever and the darkest brown hair and the most beautiful brown eyes. I first saw her in the cafeteria. I asked Johnny, "Who is that? I've never seen her before. Is she a new student?"

Johnny's reply was, "It's just a girl, and I've never seen her either." The strange thing was that after that day, every time I turned the corner, she would be there.

One day, Walter said in what I thought was the loudest voice possible, "Why don't you go ask her what her name is?"

"Shh!" I said, in what was possibly just as loud. "Tinsley Nathaniel won't, he's chicken."

Then Walter made a life-changing statement. "Maybe Tinsley needs to become someone else. You need to become more confident and speak for yourself."

As we live from day to day, we discover that certain people tend to have great influence over who we become, both in our personality and the names others know us by. When I met Audrey Rochelle Simpson, today's Nate Thomas became a reality.

A couple of days later, I saw her in the hall by a set of lockers, and with every bit of courage I could find, I went up to her and said, "Hi!" and coughed to clear my throat. When I attempted to say something else, this squeaky voice came out, so as I began to turn away, I heard her say "Hi!". You would think that I had just spoken to a celebrity by the way I felt and acted. Then, it happened. I opened my mouth and said, "I'm Tinsley Nathaniel Thomas, but you can call me Nate." And behold- Nate Thomas came alive! Little did I know at that time; I had just met the love of my life and the future Audrey Rochelle Simpson (Thomas).

My parents had planned this birthday party for me since I was like ten years old. They knew that turning thirteen was special, but I thought that I might be getting too old for such a thing. I told my mom "I'm too old for birthdays." She quickly said, "Tinsley, if you stop having birthdays, you're dead. You're not, so that settles it."

Out of frustration, I said "You know what I mean. I just don't want to be treated like a kid." "Tinsley, you are my kid, and I love you," she said with a smile. Giving in, I said, "I love you too, Mom."

My birthday that year happened to be a Saturday, and it was and still is April 1. Wasn't I lucky to have been born on April Fool's Day? I was told to be sure and invite all my "close" friends.

Since Johnny knew of my meeting Audrey, he said, "Why not invite Audrey to your party?"

I should have used the excuse that she wasn't as of yet, a close friend, but instead I responded to his bold statement, "But Johnny, she's a girl."

With a big smile on his face, he said, "And so are Ann, Debra, Diane, and Carol."

"Well, you know what I meant." That was my way of saying that I would have to ask her and face the possibility of her telling me "No." Much to my surprise, she said, "Yes, let me check with my mom, but it shouldn't be a problem. She wants me to meet and make new friends."

The party was in our backyard, and the sun was shining like someone had just turned on a huge outdoor light. There was a slight breeze, which kept the temperature down some. Johnny knew a band that a cousin of his contacted. They were just getting set up and tuned. My mom had said, "You can have a band as long as they don't get too loud and bother the neighbors, much." Some of our youth from church were invited and were there, as well as Bro. Jimmy and Mrs. Pam. One thing I recall was that as it was in April, it was strange to hear both Beach Boy's and Jan and Dean music which made us yearn for the summer. The party was fun, and we were grateful to be creating more memories together.

Besides, I got to know Audrey better and shared her with my friends.

At the age of thirteen, I had a lot of growth to do both physically and mentally. That included spiritually and developing plain common sense. It seems though that being called Nate meant that I had to allow responsibility to enter my life. I now had to impress others beside my parents. Of course, as I got older, I learned that ultimately God came first and all else was to fall in place. As I reflect on those earlier years, I find it easier to accept my position in life as a husband, friend, son, and teacher/writer. I thank people like Audrey who have that kind of influence.

That next week after the party, Johnny made a point to tell me something he felt couldn't wait any longer. "Tin-Man, I apologize for the comments I made when you first noticed Audrey. She is more than just a girl. As far as I am concerned, she is one of us. She is pretty and fun to be around. I guess you can forget about that crush you had on Miss Chapel."

"I agree on what you just said, but it may be too soon to forget about that crush completely, but thanks" and I sincerely said, "I'm glad you feel that way!"

That year school was winding down quickly. We had just learned that a major project had been assigned in science and would be entered into the school's science fair. Johnny and I agreed to work as partners to help each other with their projects. Johnny's would be on fire prevention and, and mine would be a presentation of how science supports creation by a Creator/God. Talk about taking a chance. So, the clock was ticking as I got out my encyclopedias and most definitely, my Bible.

CHAPTER 17
THE *BIG* PROJECT

All of our science classes had two weekends preparing our projects for presentations. Each class would then select two projects to represent them at the science fair. Each project would be graded on imagination, skill, and perseverance. *Imagination* meant how much thought and effort went into the planning of it. *Skill* referred to the level of difficulty. *Perseverance* showed how dedicated you were to complete the task at hand. Each student would receive a grade in class. Only a final A would make the project eligible for consideration for the science fair. A panel of independent judges would pick the top three projects at the science fair, and they would be awarded the prizes provided by the community.

It was quite exciting to be involved in such an event, except for those with absolutely no interest at all in science. Some of us definitely had a problem with motivation. Johnny and I had that covered, since we said that we would help each other. Ann asked Johnny to help her, but he had already committed himself to work with me. So, she planned to spend a lot of time in the library. We knew she most likely had another plan in her mind that included a certain boy. Bruce figured he could find a way to assist his native people, so he would do quite a bit of research. Walter headed to meet Pastor Jimmy and others from our church. Debra and Diane planned to work together, while Ken'eth wasn't at all sure, but thought he could get it done. Carol had already been reading up on a subject that she felt good about.

As a teacher, I now know the importance each student places on family and friends. When trying to learn new things and reaching goals, it helps to make the effort to meet new people and to develop meaningful relationships.

To make my point, just a few weeks before our science project, another new student came to our school. One day after school, Johnny came running up as if he was on his way to a fire. "Where's the fire?", I asked.

Johnny, all out of breath, said, "Did you hear? A new girl has come to town and enrolled in school. She had lived in South Carolina. Her name is Patricia Renee Newberry. She apparently grew up in a small town a little more than an hour from Charleston. No one knows much more, except that her family was once wealthy. I was told that she appeared to be rather snooty and that she was a science nerd. A teacher was heard saying that she might be the one to beat in the science fair."

It certainly seemed to me that this Miss Newberry would present a challenge. I still felt ready and well prepared until the day we met. There she was all dressed real proper like. She had her hair pulled back behind her ears. She was wearing a pair of pink sunglasses.

As soon as she saw me, she said, "You must be Tinsley Nathaniel Thomas, the smart science nerd that I'm supposed to be so concerned about." To be a gentleman, I stretched out my hand to shake hers. She reacted by telling me, "Look, you do your best work, and I'll do mine. We'll save the so-called friendly stuff till after the science fair." After that, she turned and went about her business.

Johnny and I got right on our projects. All our friends agreed that we should postpone any of our normal activities. I figured that I was ahead because of my encyclopedia set. Johnny had been working on his subject for several weeks due to his ongoing interest in fire prevention. All I needed to do was finish finding my evidence that supported how science and various studies showed truths in what was considered creation theories. Many Biblical accounts mention places and that many findings were documented. Even though I would have liked to, I didn't actually have to prove anything. I only had to do a thorough job of presenting the information so that if I wanted it could be used in a debate setting. The only other item needed was some sort of hands-on presentation that would get the viewer involved.

As the many days and nights went by working on our projects, it finally came to the day to gather it all and bring it to class. Our science teacher had tables set up in the back of the classroom for our projects.

Walter was almost late getting his turned in due to a problem with Ken'eth and his project. He told us, "I almost wanted to strangle my brother for making us late, but I couldn't because he was so upset and worried about it. We were told that we could come by the science classroom after school to find out our grades. The announcement of which two projects would represent each class would be made on Monday afternoon of next week.

All of us guys talked about going fishing to get our minds off the coming results, but we just couldn't settle down long enough to organize the outing. Johnny had suggested that we rest at home with our families and meet at the church Sunday morning and just give it over to God.

So as planned, we were in our places for Sunday School. Our lesson was on the miracles of Jesus, of which we felt we could use one. We sang about letting our light shine before our fellow man.

Naturally, Walter wondered why we were to shine our light only for men. "Don't females have to see where they are going?" I believe that he was actually trying to get us to smile, because he was smiling when he said it.

When Monday morning came along, none of us was late to school and we were eager to get the results for our projects. We had been told that each project had been awarded ribbons. All A's had blue ribbons, B's had red ribbons, C's had white ribbons, and D's had gray ones. If you didn't have a ribbon, you failed. From what we were told, if you turned in a project, you didn't fail. In our class, we had eight A's. Johnny and I were two of them. The rumor was, and it was a loud rumor, that Patricia Newberry was one of the A's in her class. It would be later that day when we would find out which two from each class would go on to the science fair.

As we all headed toward the classroom that afternoon, Carol came running up to us in quite a happy mood. She said, "My project was one of those selected, isn't that great", then she realized what that meant. I looked at Johnny and said,

"That means that only one of us still has a chance of representing our class in the fair."

As we entered the room, I saw my project sitting on the teacher's desk. I figured that after all that work, it paid off, but Johnny's project apparently wasn't chosen. As I turned toward him to say something, he was already shaking my hand, and with a big smile said, "I'm so happy yours got selected. I'm still happy anyway. I got an A and that might not have happened without your help."

The day of the science fair arrived. The ladies with the P.T.A. were there. They had planned to take advantage of an opportunity for a membership drive and to sell concessions to raise funds. There were twenty-four entries. Every project was grade-A quality, many of them would generate community interest. I know now from experience that great ideas don't just come from adults or from businesses and corporations.

The committee of judges had arrived and was already examining each project that was on display. Each student was required to be with their entry in case of questions and to give any demonstrations as needed.

Our newest classmate, Patricia Renee Newberry, and her project were attracting a lot of attention. It apparently had to do with all the basics and workings of science. It had what looked like atoms and molecules and many working parts. It was very colorful and even made some sort of buzzing sound. Gathered around it were several adults whom I didn't know besides the project committee. I thought that looked rather suspicious.

The time for the big announcement had come. Our gang of friends were gathering around Carol and me. Even my newest friend Audrey was right there supporting us.

The committee named the top twelve projects and began announcing those participants so as to have them come forward. They were named in alphabetical order according to our last names. As they reached the B's, they said, "Carol Louise Benjamin." Our group and others hollered out their joy for her. As they went through the N's, something within me didn't want to hear it…but they said, "Patricia Renee Newberry." Along came the T's, and yes indeed, they said, "Tinsley Nathaniel Thomas."

Of course, everyone seemed happy. The truth was that a lot of great projects were being presented, and anyone could be the top pick.

Walter, of course, decided to make his prediction which didn't sit well with Carol. "I honestly can't see how any girl could possibly beat your project, Tinsley." I bet that lump on his head lasted a while.

The final project participants were once again asked to stand by their projects. Mr. Malone was the chairman of the committee, so he announced, "The winner of third place is Billy E. Wallace." The crowd went crazy, even though very few knew who Billy was. Then things got intense. They shocked everyone by telling them that they would announce the top two winners together and for me and Patricia to remain behind our projects. That meant… You could hear an imaginary drum roll.

Mr. Malone announced, "The winner of second place is… Tinsley Nathaniel Thomas, and first place goes to our newest student, Patricia Renee Newberry."

All I recall hearing was Walter saying, "Tinsley got beat by a girl!"

CHAPTER 18

LOVE, FLOWERS, AND KINDNES

Life in those early days in Johnny's World had many learning experiences as you would expect with children. As you can imagine, I did learn how to trust new people. I learned to fish. I became more confident in who I was becoming. I also learned how to love. Oh yes, Tinsley Nathaniel Thomas became Mr. TNT, but not without a lot of fizzles.

My present-day wife, the former Audrey Rochelle Simpson, would agree with me that our falling in love had found a few speedbumps along the way. That first day I saw her in the school cafeteria, it was as if a light switch had been flipped on. I guess you could call it love at first sight. If you asked Audrey about that day, she would probably say, "When and where was this?"

Even if "love at first sight" did happen, she would deny it. The day I approached her at the lockers was to me "special". She says, "I was curious about this small-framed four-eyed boy who seemingly wasn't afraid to talk with a girl whom he never met and ask her to come to his thirteenth birthday party. It was even possible that he didn't have many friends, so I said yes. What I soon learned was that he was a very trusting boy who was admired by many and that I was the only one in the whole world that knew him as *Nate*." Wow!

I recall one day after school, probably on a Friday. It was in the fall of the year after I first met Audrey. The guys and a few other friends were playing around before football tryouts. Some of the girls, including Audrey and even Patricia Newberry, were sitting on nearby bleachers. I wasn't very athletic, but I never usually tell the guys no when it comes to having fun, like throwing the ball around. Every time I played ball; I had to remove my eyeglasses.

Johnny was quarterbacking, and Walter was center. We all ran out for a pass, and right at the moment Johnny threw me the ball, Audrey yelled "Go Nate!" Naturally, I looked in her direction instead of keeping my squinting eyes on the ball. It hit me right in the face. Grabbing my face with both hands, I discovered a bloody nose. Right about then, as the guys were about to check on me, the coaches came out and called those who were trying out. They noticed my bloody nose and immediately sent me to the trainer for medical attention. By the time I got out with gauze taped on my nose that covered what seemed to be half my face, no one was around.

Come Monday morning, everyone wanted to know why I wasn't in church. I said, "My nose was so swollen, and my face bruised that I didn't want to deal with all the questions and the embarrassment." That's when I saw Audrey and her response surprised me. She said, "I didn't know you got hurt. As soon as you missed that pass, we left. I'm sorry. If I had noticed, I would have stayed with you." At that comment, she planted a kiss on my forehead that happened not to have gauze covering it.

"Thank you, I feel better already." I said.

One person I haven't shared much about was Johnny's sister, Ann. By the time she was fourteen, she spent most of her time either at Dorman's Quick Stop, where her boyfriend, Bruce Mayfield worked, or at his house where he lived with his parents. On the day she turned sixteen, she began working at the Quick Stop. Even though Bruce was her motivation for hanging there, she had got quite an inside look at the retail and grocery business. Today, they are happily married and are running a successful supermarket in a neighboring city.

Speaking of "Bruce", our good friend Bruce "Fish-Man" Lightfoot once planted a huge garden *of forget-me-nots* all because a girl named Lucy Lewis told him she loved the flower. A great grandfather of his once said, "the spirits will often make someone's innermost thoughts come to pass if he is sincere with all his heart." Bruce was convinced that Lucy loved the flower literally because she didn't want him to ever forget her. So, in the name of love and flowers, he aimed to prove it to be true. Within just a few weeks, Lucy and her family had moved to Arizona, where *forget-me-nots* might find it a struggle to grow and a garbage truck ran over Bruce's flowers, which he hasn't forgotten.

Times when Walter got bopped in the head for remarks made about a girl repeated itself many times, and Carol has been on the delivery end most of the time. One time Walter had planned to take Carol as his date to a church Sweetheart Banquet. He sent her a handwritten letter inviting her, and she accepted. He had sent her roses two days prior and had even arranged a huge corsage to be delivered on the day of the banquet. On the day of the banquet, he had a phone call from one of her cousins telling him that she had had an accident at home. She broke her big toe on her right foot and couldn't wear a shoe. So, what did Walter do? He went over to her house early, helped her soak her foot, wrapped it and provided a comfortable shoe-like slipper and escorted her to the banquet. I believe his head bops have been much fewer since then.

I would be leaving out an important part of the Pastor Jimmy and Mrs. Pam story if I didn't take a moment to share their last days as our Pastor. When the church first learned of Pastor Jimmy's resignation, the basic reaction was, "Oh no, what will we do?" They were an important part of our church for what seemed like a very long time. "The church will fall apart and what about those children and youth. They may all leave." As soon as Reverend Jimmy had shared the details of his upcoming departure, we had the parents of some of the younger children step up and volunteer to take over in the children's department during the interim. Also, one of the older boys volunteered to be a leader as well. Naturally, they would be quite difficult to replace since they had been at our church for ten years. Our church announced a going-away party for the Johnson's and invited their adult daughter and grandchildren to participate. We wanted to be certain that they would remember our love for them and that we wished them well in their next ministry opportunity. So, very few people were surprised when it was revealed that Walter Davidson had volunteered to give a speech during the party.

Walter was becoming quite a speaker. He had always had the gift of gab, of which wasn't always a good thing. To sum it up, he said, "Reverend Jimmy, you and Pam have always been such an inspiration to us all. To me, you have been a mentor. Some of you may not know this, but I have surrendered to the call to become a minister. I will be attending college and eventually the cemetery. Ha! I gotcha! No, of course I mean the seminary." As usual, everyone laughed but clapped with joy in their hearts. Walter then announced, "Let's have all those who were a child or youth during their ministry to stand." More than half of those were standing there. Walter went on to say, "You may have noticed all the roses in here. As a token of our love for you both, each of us kids have purchased a red rose for you. At last count, we have 101 roses. We salute you and your dedication that you gave each of us these past ten years!"

To say the least, Brother Jimmy was speechless for once, and, as I recall, a song comes to mind: "Love Is in the Air!" It certainly was.

CHAPTER 19

REPORT THE FACTS, MA'AM!

Appleton has had its share of excitement through the many years that I have lived here. One of the biggest was an incident that took place just before we arrived. The buzz over it was still everywhere.

The road into town from the north has a bridge that allows traffic to cross Apple Creek. Most of the time, very little water runs under it. This time, things were very different. For many years, the facts of this incident have been made into what some call a tale. This story isn't one to share around a campfire, although it has. This story was real, and it is about someone who grew up in Appleton.

Sandra Jones was the daughter of Jed and June Jones. June had passed several years earlier. Sandra loved her parents deeply. Even though Jed was struggling to keep the farm and make it productive, things were changing. Sandra had received a great job offer in a city about an hour away. She couldn't pass up such an opportunity. She had promised to keep in touch. Jed was okay with it for a while, but he was lonely. He tried to get her to commute, which she tried. Driving became too much of a chore daily and the costs of an apartment and the gas and everything else added up.

Sandra decided to tell Jed of her plans to move away on his sixtieth birthday. She hosted a party at the house with friends and some relatives. After the last guest left, she motioned him to sit in his favorite chair. "Dad," she said, "I have found a house near my job and plan to move out soon."

Immediately, his face showed disappointment and worry. "Sandra," he said, "are you sure you have thought this through? You are leaving me all by myself. How do you expect me to take care of the farm alone?"

She then said, "It is time for me to focus more on my needs, and I promise to keep in touch.

Besides, you have friends who would love to give you a hand when you are in need."

Many days went by and eventually turned into weeks. From time to time, she would call but seldom would he answer. The only time he would call her was on her birthday and the call would be brief. Those weeks added up to months and then years.

On that day, a day Jed will never forget, the skies grew dark, and the sun refused to shine. He had spent the morning going through old photos and spoke out loud to June and he could imagine her answering back. "Now Jed, you know this thing with Sandra has gone on long enough. You need to give her a call, and you know what needs to be said."

Rain had already been falling for the last seven days, some of which were downpours. During one of those early downpours, Jed got up the nerve to call his daughter. All he got was a message and a beep, so he left a long, emotional message pleading her to forgive him and to, "please forgive my selfish attitude and to come visit soon, that is if you *can* forgive me."

Later that day, Jed decided that he'd better try to get the cows to come in since they weren't able to see well enough to do it on their own. It was definitely going to be a stormy night. If Jed didn't get the herd in soon, some could get injured or worse. Suddenly, there was a loud burst of thunder, followed by a lightning strike that scared him to the bone. As he gathered his senses, another lightning strike happened; this one was flash lightning. He thought he had seen a car's headlights about to come down the hill that approached the bridge.

As you are coming in from the north, there is a hairpin curve at the top of the hill. As you approach the curve, the speed drops to 45 miles per hour. As you go down the hill, it decreases to 35 to prepare you for the bridge. The bridge itself is narrow, allowing only one car at a time to cross. A yield sign is posted at the entrance of the bridge on each side.

During that flash of lightning, Jed expected to see the car either crossing or coming off the bridge. It wasn't. The time was 11:59 P.M. He had just gathered the last of the herd and was headed back home. As he quickly entered the house, he saw that the old clock on the wall said 12:01. He thought that was the quickest two minutes ever, then he remembered that when they have severe lightning the electricity in the house cuts out for a bit and usually comes back on almost immediately.

The rain was getting worse, so he decided to go to bed and try to get some rest.

The next morning, the rain slowed down, and the darkness was fleeing. Jed felt he needed to go check the bridge. He hadn't seen his daughter in five years, and he wasn't expecting company either, but he felt uneasy. Earlier he had called the police chief, Sam Worthington, to report a possible car that might be missing after not making it across the bridge during the night's storm.

As Jed got to the bridge, he noticed the guardrail was busted and more damage was noticeable to the bridge itself. About that time, two dispatched police cars were arriving.

After a thorough look, a car was found lodged underneath the bridge up against some timbers that had been washed there. The current was fierce, so they had to use ropes to get a man down to the car. The driver's door was open, and nobody was found. After a thorough search of the car, they found identification in the glove compartment. The car belonged to Sandra Jones. The only thing Jed could figure was that Sandra had gotten his heartfelt message and just couldn't wait to see him. That meant she had forgiven him!

Our dear friend Walter once around a campfire shared this story, but in search of another bop on the head, added something. "The thing is," Walter said, "You know, no one ever found a body and sometimes you can be out down by the bridge and might hear a faint, 'Help me, please, help me.'" That's Walter for ya!

I'm sure most people have heard of *Ripley's Believe It or Not!* Well, Appleton has what I would call one such story. It happened during my senior year at Appleton High. Our football team was the Wildcats. That year, we had done well with a 7-4 record going into the final game with the three-time high school champ Ashton Bobcats. Johnny, Ken'eth, and Walter played on that team. Johnny played receiver, Ken was a cornerback and Walter was center. Diane Davidson's boyfriend was Todd Jenkins, the team quarterback. We also had a running back named Earl Kamp, who went on to play in the NFL. I worked with the team trainer.

The remarkable thing about our team was that we had just enough players to qualify to play the game. Some had to play offense and defense. During that year, we had two of our boys who played linemen on both offense and defense. Because of responsibilities at home with their farm, they had to drop out in mid-season leaving us with just enough players to play.

During the first half alone, we had players carried off the field hurting, only to have them limp back in after time-outs. At half-time, the score was 14-0 with the Bobcats in the lead. During that break, we learned that two of our linemen were in bad shape and would not be able to return. That would mean that we would be forced to forfeit the game. Now, I don't understand everything about football, but it seemed to me that our two linemen that left earlier in the season were never replaced; they had only vacated their positions. I told the coach and said, "Coach, someone told me they were here and really wished they could help. Why don't we send someone to the officials and ask if instead of forfeiting such an important game, we just send these two guys in as subs?" We did, they agreed, and the other team agreed.

Now, I'm quite certain the Bobcats from Ashton believed they had this game easily, considering how the first half went. After the "subs" had their pads and jerseys on, they were escorted to the field to join the rest of the team. The crowd on our side went bananas. One thing the other team might not have thought about was that our players were fresh, new the plays and were leaders. Our crowd also acted as catalysts to excite our players. Our lines began to work as units. On offense, Todd was more accurate with his passing and Earl found holes to run through. Even Johnny got his share of catches. The score was tied at 14, with fifty-two seconds remaining. It looked like a tie was possible unless we kicked a field goal, and that really hadn't been an option all season. So, on third down and nine yards to go, Todd handed the ball to Earl. Quiet was the sound, and behind one of our farmer boys was Earl Kamp to the rescue. "Touchdown" was the call, and the extra point was good. The Bobcats couldn't get another first down after the kickoff and as the clock ran down, we had our believe it or not moment. Appleton Wildcats 21, Ashton Bobcats 14.

I almost forgot one. During our first county fair after our arrival, a lady named Shirley Minard, known to most as Aunt Shirley, entered the pie contest as she had done many times before. She didn't always win but often placed in the top three. This was a year she felt confident so she was bragging everywhere she went about how she would win. The time had come, and all the contestants were there as the crowd gathered.

Suddenly, there was a scream. It was Aunt Shirley. "Where's my pie?" she cried. "It's missing!

One of those poor losers has stolen it so I won't win."

As usual, there was always a policeman at public events. Officer Malone was on the scene quickly. As soon as he arrived, he told the distraught Aunt Shirley, "Report the facts ma'am!"

Well officer, the facts are quite clear. One of these people has obviously taken my prize-winning pie!

"Yes Ma'am, I will immediately look into it!" said Officer Malone. Shortly afterward, the officer returned. "Mrs. Minard, do you have a nephew named Jake?"

"Well yes," she responded, looking puzzled. The officer then brought to her a boy with every bit of evidence all over his face.

"Blueberry, I suppose?" said the Policeman.

"And it was very good!" confessed Jake.

So, these were the top stories of excitement in our Appleton, at least for now. The future was on its way very quickly, and there was no way I could have been prepared for all of it!

CHAPTER 20

THOSE WERE THE DAYS, MY FRIEND!

As I, Nate Thomas, sit here typing away, these are more than words on paper. They are life itself. My life. Johnny's life. Even your life. These were the days…of MY Johnny's World. A world of friendship, of kindness, of acceptance. Those were the days of beginnings and lifelong relationships.

Was it a day when a child and his family moved from a place of familiarity to a life of uncertainty? Was it a day of making friends, as awkward as it might have been? Could it have been a day at the park or a day holding a fishing pole, just waiting for that BIG one to come along?

Days filled with anticipation. Days wondering when the rain would end, and the sun would shine again. One of those days I recall was the day of my graduation from Appleton High School. It was a day in May. The sun was shining as bright as a wishful "almost" summer day could be. We had all gathered in the school cafeteria to get our gowns and funny-looking caps or hats or whatever they were. They really didn't fit every head, regardless of what the label said.

Our Principal, Mrs. Moore, was testing out the megaphone to make sure it would grate on everyone's nerves. She was successful. She and other members of her staff were trying their best to get us all in what they thought would be alphabetical order, until another latecomer showed up, causing more confusion. I could see why they wanted us to be there two hours before time to begin.

The plan was to march out the eastside doors of the cafeteria. We would then head toward the stadium, which was due west. As soon as we reached the eastside gates, we were instructed to wait for the signal to proceed toward the podium area. The only problem appeared to be that no one seemed to be sure of the signal. Some thought it was going to be Mrs. Moore on the megaphone. Others said they heard that it would be when the music starts. I wondered if it really mattered.

Just before we began to get in our final order in the stands, each of our "gang" friends gave each other a wave or thumbs up. Of course, Johnny gave me a high five. Bruce added a nod of the head.

Carol did her best bow while temporarily losing her cap. Walter did what I believe was a jump, skip, and a hop that ended with a complete spin. What can I say? It was Walter.

The signal was apparently a squeal from the megaphone, because that is what we all heard before the music began. The official word on how many seniors were graduating was 259. How was that even possible? Later, we learned that the high school boundaries had included the farming community outside of the normal boundary lines.

All of a sudden, the music stopped briefly and a voice I knew was Walter Davidson's voiced a prayer. "Heavenly Father, we thank you for bringing us together today to celebrate and to move forward on the path you have given each of us. We say a special thanks to parents and teachers for getting us here and Hallelujah, we made it!"

The order of events to follow were the singing of our school song and the traditional march to receive our diplomas and throwing our lovely caps unofficially into the air.

After the ceremony, we five and our families and close friends met at the church, mainly because there were others from church who graduated. Our little group had been sharing our plans and goals for some time. Johnny was headed to a two-year college followed by fire school to get his certification to be a fireman. Bruce planned to attend a nearby college to study law. He was particularly interested in becoming an advocate for Native Americans. Walter was headed to a local college and then a seminary to become a pastor. Carol had plans to attend a nearby college with hopes of working for a local newspaper. She and Walter were getting much closer, even though he wouldn't call it an engagement just yet.

What about Tinsley Nathaniel Thomas? I had continued to date Audrey. After spending much of my time assisting Johnny with various ideas and dreams for fire prevention, I decided it was time for me to pursue my future. Science was still a top interest of mine. I figured I would enroll in a college with a strong science department with the goal of becoming a science teacher. As you well know, writing has also become an interest. I enjoy recalling the things in life that make it what it is: people, places, and staying true and honest with those you cross paths with.

It looked like some of our friends and acquaintances that make up Johnny's World may be going in different directions, but as life continues, so does our story. What do you suppose is in store for our Johnny's World?

Part three: JOHNNY'S WORLD… *Life Goes On*

CHAPTER 21
WHAT'S NEXT?

As I sit here reminiscing, I can remember it as if it were yesterday. Yes, you can imagine how life after High School was becoming quite a whirlwind. Waking up to the clanging of that alarm clock, announcing that first day of college. I had a feeling of great anticipation as I hurried through my morning routine and headed to the breakfast table.

I heard mom's voice immediately, "Tinsley, you found the clothes I laid out for you?"

"Yes mom, but you don't have to do that for me. I'm in college."

"But Tinsley, I want you to look your absolute best. You know what they say about first impressions!"

I really did appreciate everything my mother did for me, because I knew it was out of genuine love. She had to get to work as well. As I took that last swallow of juice, I headed out the door and to the 1973 Volkswagen dad had got me. It was a deep shamrock-like green. It took me a while to adjust to the standard transmission, with all the "pop the clutch and shift." Sometimes, the whole car would shake! I had to pick up Bruce Lightfoot and Walter Davidson on my way.

Walter called minutes before I left saying, "Tinsley, where are you?" I told him, "" I'll be there, don't rush me. Go eat a bug or something." Walter answered as only he could, "Na, I already had my Wheaties and toast."

Bruce hoped to get a law degree, but this semester he was taking general courses. Walter was going to head towards a sociology degree and then on to the seminary. As for me, I hoped to get a degree in Secondary Education with a specialization in science.

The drive to the college was about twenty miles away. I realized that a "Bug" was not the most comfortable vehicle to travel in, especially if you are in the backseat. The guys often flipped a coin to see who got to ride up front. On that day, and many since, we spent our travel time talking about many things, mostly relating to the future and daily expectations.

You might wonder why I have not mentioned Johnny Sampson. A week earlier, he checked into Dodge City Community College in Kansas. Their school motto is "In Quest of Truth." He planned to get a two- year degree and move on to attend the Texas Fireman's Training School at Texas A&M. He planned to get his Firefighters Certification. We were all incredibly happy for him and had wished him tons of luck with a huge party. All the gang came and then some.

As we pulled into a parking place, we heard a loud noise down from us. It was made by the ugliest car we have ever seen. It had to be hand painted, literally. You could see brush strokes. We could not believe it when the door screeched open and out came Todd Jenkins, our former quarterback at Appleton. He was super proud of his "new" set of wheels.

"Hey Todd," we yelled "where did you find that beauty?"

"My dad bought it for me the last time he was home. You knew he was in the military, didn't you? He is overseas. He told me I could get it painted while he was away. We really didn't have the money to get it done professionally, so I did it myself."

We decided to leave the conversation alone so as not to hurt Todd's feelings, although Walter nearly inserted foot, thus coming close to doing just that.

As we walked through the courtyard, we saw Carol Benjamin coming toward us. I had noticed how Walter's steps picked up their pace. For the fun of it, Bruce got there just before him and gave her a big hug and gave Walter the biggest grin.

"Hey, hands off fella" as he laughed aloud. The four of us continued together until we had to go separate ways to find our individual classes.

That first week was pretty normal, as college classes go. All four of us, including Johnny, settled into the life of college students. Ann Sampson, Johnny's sister, continued to work at Dorman's Quick Stop, along with her boyfriend Bruce Mayfield.

Debra Davidson graduated from High School five years earlier, so she had been working as an office aid at City Hall. She had nearly completed her accounting/ business degree.

Diane Davidson could not wait to graduate from High School and get married to Todd, the love of her life. The only thing she did not like about him was his new hand-painted car, but she forced herself to accept it. Oh, how he loved that car.

Now, Ken'eth Davidson (yep, that was his college way of spelling his name, although he continues to spell it with a dash as well) was one we all could not understand. Somehow, during High School, Sue Worthington caught his eye and held it tightly until he proposed. We had reminded him how she and her brother Billy had caused so much trouble after the Miller Fire, but love IS blind. One other thing just as important was his aspiration to become a lawyer. College was ahead of him, as well as law school.

Johnny spent most of his time in Kansas once he began his two years at Junior College. Before that, he worked and received training for nearly three years at the fire station in Appleton.

Okay, so you are wondering what became of a lovely girl named Audrey. Yes, she was still in the picture. She was attending college locally and was majoring in Elementary Education/Music & Fine Arts. We were "for sure" dating each other. We were all asking the question, "What's next?" and my goodness, it was not at all what we had imagined!

CHAPTER 22
WEDDING BELLS!

Furthering our education and supporting our future was utmost on our agendas. I recall one day when Walter just could not wait to tell everyone the "News" about his sister Diane.

"You guys," he said sounding like an easterner. "Diane has done it now!"

"Done what?" said Bruce with a curious look on his face.

"She ran off with Todd Jenkins and got married. Can you believe it?"

Our response was "Yes!" We were more surprised at his reaction than at the news itself. We all knew how the two of them were earlier on, especially during High School. Diane was Walter's youngest sister. Even though that fact was true, Walter was less than 15 months older than her. Debra Elaine Davidson, the oldest sibling, was a week past five years older than him. It looked like she had decided not to marry, thus making Walter over-protective where Diane was concerned.

The actual story was that one evening Todd had come over to join the family for supper. They both had agreed to tell the family during the desert. They assured everyone that Diane was not pregnant. They just wanted to go somewhere romantic and get married there. Mrs. Davidson could not believe it at first. Mr. Davidson had to speak up on Diane's behalf and said, "If this is really what you both want, go ahead but let us pay for the trip and your hotel stay."

Several weeks later, Walter informed me that the honeymooners were back and had found an apartment in a nearby community for now. They hoped to buy a house eventually. The main problem Walter had now was that Diane allowed Todd to take his self-painted car on the honeymoon.

Another little surprise was the phone call I received one day from Johnny shortly after he moved to Dodge City to attend Community College. The phone rang several times. My mom would normally get it, but she was doing laundry and probably did not hear the ring. I ran quickly and got it before the caller could hang up. It was Johnny.

"Have you seen my sister Ann lately?

"Not really," I said.

Johnny went on to explain. "Mom said that yesterday Ann had spent a lot of time in her room. She could hear a lot of noises that were coming from the room, so since she hardly ever cleaned her room without being told, she was curious. When asked about the noises, she said she was doing some late spring cleaning." He went on to explain that later that day Ann came out and told mom that she was going down to the Quick Stop to meet her boyfriend Bruce Mayfield who would be getting off from work soon. As she walked toward the door to leave, she said "Love you, mom!" A few minutes later Mrs. Sampson went into Ann's room to find an open window and her suitcase gone along with several of her belongings.

"Tin-Man, they eloped! Can you believe it? My sister, who never did anything wrong, ran off and got married. She could have had the decency to at least inform our parents of their intent. I have to pray hard about this and Tinsley Nathaniel, please pray for our family."

As I hung up the phone, it occurred to me that Johnny had for the first time called me something other than Tin-Man.

Marriage---what a strange word to hear concerning our "gang." The subject did not come up a great deal during those years since we pulled into our neighborhood. *Johnny's World* was changing, and nothing was going to alter that fact.

One marriage that did not sneak up and surprise us was our colorful friends Walter and Carol. After graduation from High School, the subject came up often and plans were made. My girlfriend Audrey Rochelle Simpson and Patricia Renee Newberry had volunteered to help plan and be in the wedding. The couple had agreed on a September wedding, so the wedding was set during Walter's final year of college. The location would obviously be the First Central Baptist Church of Appleton. Our "new" pastor had been there nearly three years. His name was Allen Blake Carter. His wife's name was Cynthia Gail Carter. They had a little girl they had adopted named Josie.

The wedding was well attended. I was honored to be Walter's best man. Johnny and Bruce Lightfoot were opposite Debra Davidson and Patricia Newberry. Audrey was Carol's maid of honor. Walter and Carol wrote their vows, but Carol asked the Reverend Carter to read them for her and she would nod in agreement. Walter had no problem with his vows and no, he did not do any flips or cartwheels.

The next wedding from within our "gang" of friends came a little over a year after Walter & Carol's. The past six months after their wedding I spent a lot of time working with Johnny on fire prevention programs. He was all set to take his first three tests toward receiving his certification from the Texas A&M Fire Academy. After discussing at length with Audrey, we decided it was time to focus attention on our future together. Our wedding plans had been delayed, so it did not take much to pick up where we left them. So, we planned to get married in the Fall.

The leaves on the trees were turning colors and many were beginning to fall to the ground. There was a slight crispness in the night air. Our wedding was set for a Saturday evening. Our church was filling quickly. Johnny Sampson was my best man, and Patricia Newberry was Audrey's maid of honor. Who would have thought, Miss Know-it all Newberry in my wedding! She had become a good friend to us both.

Pastor Carter conducted the wedding ceremony and Walter had the privilege of singing. Thanks to that campfire singing we had experienced; we knew Walter could play guitar and sing. I had requested a popular song for him to sing after I said, "I do." It would be Debbie Boone's "You Light Up My Life." Audrey picked out another popular song for Walter to sing for me. It was Kenny Nolan's "I like Dreamin'." Walter was not disappointed, and neither were we.. Our Pastor was most nervous due to a migraine headache. He was in such pain that he forgot to queue us when it was time to kiss. Everyone thought it was funny that I would hesitate at such a time.

The last of our "gang" to get married was Walter's youngest brother Ken'eth. This one was a BIG shock to most in the community. For a long time, Appleton's City Prosecutor was Sam Worthington, and the Police Chief was his brother Carl Worthington. Sam had two children, Billy & Sue, with whom we had a not so "good" relationship. They almost got Johnny sent to prison with false accusations. Ken'eth first noticed a change in Sue while they were in Middle School. She was no longer that silly pain in the side kid. Ken'eth admitted that she "looked" like a "girl." It was a cool night in September. High School graduation had come and gone, and he was attending college locally with a career in Law as his goal. Sue had told him that if he timed it right, he might get her dad's position as city prosecutor.

The wedding ceremony was held at city hall in the courthouse, thanks to Sue's father. Everyone's alarm clock went off earlier than usual for a Saturday. It was expected that the turnout for this wedding would be larger than Walter's, due to the Worthington family. The only real concern was crowd control. The court room held quite a few people, but not like our church. One of the district judges who was a good friend of Sam Worthington had agreed to perform at the wedding ceremony. Security was provided by two court bailiffs. The prosecution and defense tables were removed to allow room for the wedding party. Folding chairs were placed in the rear of the court room.

As it came time for the wedding, without any music everyone except for the bride took their places. Surprising to all was when a bailiff stood up front and said, "All rise!"

Music to usher the bride in began. Someone had obviously pre-recorded it. Sue then entered looking quite lovely in her long white dress. You can be certain that money was not a problem with the purchase of that dress. As Sue took her place next to Ken'eth, the judge entered and hit the gavel three times and said, "You may be seated."

The wedding party consisted of Walter as best-man, Bruce was groomsman. Sue had her best friend Darla Dorman as her maid of honor and a friend named

Ellen Dillard as a bridesmaid. One thing though, was that Walter was unable to remain uneventful.

Afterall Ken'eth was his younger brother, and he was marrying Sue Worthington. As soon as we heard "You may kiss the bride," Walter pulled out a foghorn and let it rip! Sue let out the biggest scream, followed by the banging of the gavel. Everyone ended up laughing, including the judge.

Okay, I mentioned Audrey and about our future… as I explained earlier, we got married, but not until I graduated from college. We were both very committed to our futures and to each other. Life always had a way of guiding our directions and of course we knew the who and the what that guide was. Thank you, Lord!

As of this date, neither Debra Davidson nor Bruce Lightfoot has gotten married. It appears that they are both career-minded people. That sums it up. In the marriage department for those of us who gladly referred to us as part of *Johnny's World*. I know you are wondering about Johnny. No, he did not get married. His life was full enough, he had once said, just in helping others.

CHAPTER 23
WELCOME TO MY WORLD!

As I sit here typing I think of how many times, I told someone "Welcome to my world." Sometimes I was being sarcastic and other times I was super serious. Johnny Sampson did that for me many years ago. A young boy, who found himself in a new place with no direction, except for encouragement from his mom to go make friends. That is exactly what I did. I took that step of faith into the unknown.

The first thing I remember on that first day when I ran into Johnny (literally) was "Why can't you watch where you are going?" The boy that said that did not realize what he said. I only now know that I had no idea the "where" or the "how." I only know that an extended hand from one boy named Johnny changed my life and gave me meaning and a "where" to belong. Johnny Sampson was saying to me "Welcome to my world" with a friendly "can I help?"

Jim Reeves sang a song by that title of which the second part of that sentence says, "won't you come on in?" The kids and adults of Appleton became the invitees of which I will always be grateful. A welcome is more than just a word expressed. It is an open arm to become part of life itself. A boy did just that one day years ago. As Johnny Sampson offered to help us move in, he also offered a nerdy boy a place in his semi- private world we have called *"Johnny's World."*

I recall one morning when I was about twelve or so, Mom yelled out that familiar "Tinsley Nathaniel Thomas? Get in here, now!" Have you ever experienced the nerve- tingling feeling that goes to the very bottom of your feet and you know… "well, this is it? Doom and gloom have found me." The only thing is that when you get around to responding with a "what is wrong?" you get a "Oh nothing dear, just wanted to see if you were ready for breakfast?" Do not get me wrong. I know mom always wanted what was best for me, but sometimes I wondered!

My world today is full of joy knowing that I can and have helped many students with their education needs as well as guiding them along life's pathway. Now, can you get any cheesier than that? Perhaps. Recently, I was in my office at the school where I teach. I was busy typing material for a book when a knock sounded upon my door. It was a student named Stewart. His friends called him Stu. He reminded me of myself at that age.

"Mr. Thomas," he began. "How detailed should our report be on the human skeletal system?"

My response had been, "As detailed as you want, Stewart."

"Well, I was and has always been afraid to over-do it when it comes to these kinds of projects."

"Now, Stewart never be afraid to do your best in anything you attempt to do!"

The funny thing was that same week I had a different student with a different academic approach, and I gave him the same advice. One thing for sure that I learned during my early years in Appleton was that if I wanted to succeed in whatever I was doing, I had to do it with the right amount of zeal and determination, but not to walk over someone or act too righteous. God expects us to treat others as we would prefer to be treated. Back to the words of the Jim Reeves song… "miracles, I guess still happen now and then." Yes, they do and sometimes we do not realize it right away.

CHAPTER 24
WHAT A LIFE!

As I, Tinsley Nathaniel Thomas sit here writing and sharing my innermost thoughts and memories, I realize just how blessed I am to have been born to such caring parents and to have become friends with so many "friends" and "acquaintances." Yes, the world I have referred to as *Johnny's World* is mostly due to my meeting and getting to know my friend Johnny Sampson and experiencing many life-changing events.

Yes, as I ponder on the many experiences I have had since coming to Appleton, I think of God's hand in it all. For God loved the world so much that He sent His very own son to show us the way. We were created to love others.

Johnny's World was my shelter, my personal protection from my inward shortcomings. Johnny's outstretched hand was where it began and my continued relationships with the "gang," at least in my mind was what kept that fact a reality.

I cannot help but recall the day we lost my dad. He had just finished a shift at the plant and had headed home. He had worked two double shifts in the same week. The roads were wet, and it was late. The sun was setting, which caused the pavement to steam up and cast an eerie effect upon the road. As the sun finished its descent, my mom answered that unexpected knock at the door. It was a police officer with the city of Appleton, notifying us that there had been an accident involving my dad. "Ma'am, you are being asked to follow me to Appleton General. There has been an accident, and you need to see about your husband." Immediately, we followed. Mom had asked the police officer if he could have the Reverend Carter contacted so he might meet us at the Hospital.

The amazing thing about *Johnny's World* was that we did not have to contact anyone other than our Pastor. As soon as we arrived at the hospital, we started seeing friends. Most waited in the waiting areas but made sure we knew they were there.

Our Church was most certainly a blessing during our time of loss but having such a vast number of friends kept our minds from dwelling on the hurt and frustration of losing a family member of such importance to us.

The Bible reminds us that "a friend loveth at all times." Rather, be it during good times or troubled times or during a period of chastisement, a devoted friend really cares.

This circle of friends I refer to as *Johnny's World* began with the five of us. Almost immediately their siblings became a part of it, which brought the number to a total of nine. Eventually, my dear Audrey became number ten. Of course, we all had other friends and acquaintances who became important to us, but not like our "gang" of friends.

What a special blessing to have friends you can call on or talk to no matter where you may be! That brings to mind the time Johnny got ill while at the Fire Academy at A&M. He had been cooped up in his apartment for six days without contact from anyone. His friends up there were either working or had gone home to visit their families. One evening, our phone rang. It was Johnny.

In a strange 'Ostrich with its head in the sand' sound, he began "Hey… Tin-man? What-cha doin?" "Oh, not much! What-chew doin?" said I with great excitement. I sensed that he did not feel well and was bored to no end. I told him to be patient and wait a bit. I had a plan.

In the next thirty minutes or so, the conversation went something like, "Hey, Bruce?" "Yeah, Tinsley? What's goin?" would be the reply. "Johnny is sick and needs our encouragement," I would say. "Oh, I'll give him a call," would be their response.

For over an hour each of us called him and spent several minutes trying to cheer him up. It all began with my ordering a "the works" pizza that I had delivered to his apartment in the middle of all those best wishes. Isn't it great to belong to a bunch of friends like that of *Johnny's World?* What a life!

CHAPTER 25

IT JUST TAKES TIME

I recall one day the doorbell rang and on the other side of the door was Patricia Renee Newberry. "Tinsley," she said. "I know we haven't always been the best of friends, but as you know Audrey and I have been getting closer, so I thought you wouldn't mind helping me with a situation."

It had been a terribly busy and tiring day of classes, and I hadn't gotten my supper yet. Mom had saved me some food, and I had just warmed it up.

"What seems to be such a serious and urgent situation, Patricia?" "Well, Tinsley you remember Billy E. Wallace?" "Of course, Patricia. How could I ever forget the person who complicated our science projects to where I had to give you credit for a job well done. Besides, Billy deserved to be noticed."

Patricia began to explain, "Billy and I have been dating off and on for a while, but he has always had a lack of confidence and has struggled holding down a regular job. I can't get him to understand that he can do anything if he sets is mind to it."

I was surprised she had thought I could do anything to help the situation.

"Patricia, I barely knew Billy in school and besides, he was always proud and didn't like anyone to interfere. What can I do to help?"

In a very serious tone, she said "First of all, pray for him. I am afraid of what he might do. I honestly feel that we have a chance of having something special together, as long as he doesn't run from it."

"Okay, I will and is it alright to share this prayer need with our friends?"

Her response was a thankful, "Yes, please. Just do not allow it to become a gossip thing. He is a private guy and I'm not even sure of what he might say about my asking for prayer."

The first thing I did after praying for guidance was to ask Walter and Bruce Lightfoot if they would be willing to go with me to see Billy. It had been several years since we had seen him.

Walter asked, "Tinsley, what if he tells us to stay out of his business?"

"Then we will." Was my response.

I decided not to just show up, so I gave him a call. "Hello Billy. This is Tinsley Nathaniel Thomas. Remember me from school?

"Of course, I do," he said. "You're the guy Patty beat out in the science fair that first year after she moved here." Patty? *I would have to remember that and ask Patricia to explain, the next chance I got.*

"Yeah, could I and a couple of friends come by for a quick visit? We can talk old times and just share a moment together."

His response to that was an excited "but of course, that could be fun!"

So, a visit was made. We talked about old times. We let him go on and on about 'Patty' and his pet iguana. Eventually, we discussed the things that most concerned Patricia. Billy understood her concerns and admitted that he knew God had a plan for his life and that he just had not found it yet. We asked if we could pray with him before we left, and he said "yes." Wow, amazing how God's timing works.

Several months passed by before anything noticeable took place for Billy. He eventually got a decent job working in the same supermarket as Ann Sampson and her husband Bruce. He ended up managing the meat market for them.

My wife Audrey has told me on several occasions that if we had not prayed as we did for Billy and Patricia, they wouldn't have become the happily married couple they are today.

The Bible reminds us in James 5:16b(NKJV) "The effective, fervent prayer of a righteous man avails much." It takes time & prayer to see the fruits of our efforts. In this case, "love takes time."

CHAPTER 26
THE BALL BOUNCES

You have heard the old saying, 'Well that's the way the ball bounces?' Chance, coincidence, it was meant to be. In *Johnny's World* that has never really been true. We, the "gang" of *Johnny's World* have always had a strong belief or faith in God.

A few years ago, before any of us had children, we met together, each of us with our mates. My wife Audrey organized the meeting and made the necessary contacts. Our goal was to establish a support system for our families both in the present day and future. I recall that first conversation Audrey and I had.

"Tinsley, our friends have always been particularly important to you. Ever since we first met, you refer to everyone as *Johnny's World* and you know life as you know it would not be if it were not for Johnny Sampson extending that hand in friendship."

"Yes, that's right Audrey. Our world of friends is like a family." "Well, Tinsley my dear."

She was about to get serious because she never referred to me by that name. "You know, with God nothing happens by mistake. I believe He wants us all to treat each other as one big family. I propose that we come together as a group and plan out ways to stay connected and take care of us all. Before too long there will be children, and everyone will become even busier with jobs, kids and just everyday occurrences."

My reply was a sincere, "Audrey, sweetie" with a huge smile, "Are you saying that because God has had a hand in bringing us all together and you feel we should do everything we can to remain as a close-knit family?"

So indeed, we agreed.

The ball of concern, so to speak, began to bounce with my wife right on top. We all met (including Johnny). We all agreed to stay connected in every way possible and to remain a caring family no matter what.

The first thing we all had to do was define our family. We realized that God put us all together and did it with divine purpose. We did not just meet by chance. God brought my family to Appleton and to the neighborhood we now call *Johnny's World*.

Each of us met at the precise time and place as planned by our Lord, and just as we are appointed to meet and accept Him, we do the same with each other. Relationships mean relating to the other individual with a deep knowledge of who they are. I felt like I had already done that with our "gang," but each of them and all our other close friends and family needed to do the same.

As the ball bounces, so does true love. God loves us. Christ died for us while showing that love, so we must allow that love to grow within us until it is as though His peace and purpose is fulfilled.

One day when Walter and I were outside with nothing better to do than bouncing the basketball back and forth and shooting baskets, an amazing thought came to Walter.

"Hey Tinsley, you know what?" said Walter.

I answered with a smile "No, I can't read your mind completely. What?"

"Don't you think that if we are going to do exactly as God wishes that we need to ask Him a thing or two?"

Now, Walter had a knack for saying the wrong thing at the wrong time, but this time he was right on time. What he said was not a shock or anything I did not know, in fact I felt like it would have come up, but Walter beat us to it.

So, from that day on we agreed as a group that praying for each other would be our first base (stealing from the game of baseball). The second base would be keeping in touch with each other, if possible, each week. Third base would be reporting to at least one of us in the event of a personal prayer need. Of course, church attendance and a regular personal time with God was a commitment we agreed to.

I still recall the day I walked into the children's department at the church not knowing what to expect and seeing my "new" friends and having one of them actually say "Hey, sit by me." I would have to say that the ball bounced again.

That ball is one of faith, hope and reverence toward our Lord and Savior. We live by what we learn. We learn from our mistakes. As that ball of life bounces, we must be patient not to get ahead of the bounce and get rolled over. So, things do not just happen. God has a plan for each of us and yes, for certain, that includes *Johnny's World.*

CHAPTER 27

MY GOODNESS! CHILDREN!

As a writer, I have the privilege of having the first crack at a given subject. *(The writer holds the pen.)* Most people dream of having their own family when they get older. They hope to find that "someone" that God has for their mate and have children.

As for us, Nate & Audrey Thomas, the Lord has blessed us with two children. A boy named Theodore Nicholas Thomas, and a girl named Adalee Rae Thomas.

I recall a morning when I had just shaved & showered and was about to grab my tall container of coffee before going out the door.

"Nate," I heard Audrey calling.

"Yes, dear?" I replied.

In a voice mixed with joy and reluctance, she said "Nate, how do you feel about children?"

She knew very well that I liked kids and wanted our own, so I was a bit puzzled until I understood the look on her face. It was the 'I'm pregnant' look.

It was the same for our next child as it was for our first. All our friends were excited and a tremendous help during each pregnancy.

Our most colorful couple, Carol and Walter Davidson, probably topped the list.

Sometime after Walter received his Sociology degree and married our editor & chief of *The Appleton Gazette,* life sped up for those two. Carol went from one pregnancy to the next until they were proud parents of four highly active children. Their names are Wally, Carla, Eddie, and Louisa. Each child's middle initial was B for Carol's given name Benjamin.

Walter called me one evening. He and Carol had been married a bit, he said, "Tinsley, Carol is pregnant and we're on our way to that Godly number of seven and I can't wait." Originally, I thought I would have twelve since it has been said 'cheaper by the dozen,' but Carol said NO! I cannot help but think she said NO again right after the fourth!"

Ann Sampson, Johnny's Sister got married right after High School to her sweetheart Bruce Mayfield. They had quite a lot of experience in the "supermarket" industry, so moved to a nearby town and opened a grocery store. Bruce manages the meat market. After about three years Ann gave birth to their first daughter, Annie Maria. Bruce was so thrilled; his yell was her all the way back to Dorman's Quick Stop where Ann & Bruce met. Ann was so worried when the second child came because she thought Bruce would only be happy if it was a boy. Wrong! It was a girl named Brooke Skylar.

Walter's youngest sister, Diane, who married our star quarterback Todd Jenkins, had three children. As you may recall, Diane was the oldest of twins. Her first two children were twins. The first was a boy named Toby, then a girl named Dolly. Their third child, a girl named Ellie.

A while back, we had a backyard cookout in which we had it at Walter's youngest brother's place. Ken-eth & Sue had told us "Yes" right away. They had twin girls named Eagan and Keagan, and Ken-eth Jr. their only son. It is quite a surprise to see that Walter's little brother was quite a family man and with a most unlikely partner and on top of that he was the city prosecutor.

In a span of Ten years or less my *Johnny's World* increased by eighteen because of our children and that is not including any of our extended family of friends and acquaintances. Our family was full of happiness, laughter, and God's multiple blessings and not just because of our children. As I said before, Johnny Sampson, Bruce Lightfoot and Debra Davidson never married, nor had their own children.

Yet, they were always and will always be a part of the "Gang." Our children are loved and pampered by us all.

I recall one of our last get-togethers. Johnny was able to be with us and as soon as he walked in and saw all the kids running around, his words were "My Goodness! Children!"

CHAPTER 28
A LEGAL DILEMMA

Through the years, our friends have had troubles for one reason or another. It was exciting and a little troubling at times knowing that we had two lawyers in our "Gang."

Bruce "fish-man" Lightfoot eventually became a defense attorney in our county, but before that he was a legal advocate for Native Americans in our region. Ken-eth Davidson became Appleton's City Prosecutor and eventually the county prosecutor.

For quite a while, Bruce would counsel individuals in need of legal advice from the Indian population. Once he became a defense attorney, he began to get quite a few clients from his experiences with Native Americans, especially being one himself. He would often meet with representatives from AIM, the American Indian Movement legal division. Even though the group's activities had quieted considerably over the years, they still stood for the right to protect Indigenous peoples in culture, nature, and spirituality. They believed, if a need existed, the work would continue.

None of us had a problem with Bruce's work. In fact, we applauded him every chance we had. The only time there was a problem was when he would have to go up against Ken-eth which did not happen often except for the case of *Appleton County vs. Freddie Apenimon Longfellow*. As I re-visit the memory of this case, I cannot help but smile, as I remember the joy we all felt at seeing two of our very own serving their community, even though they were on opposite sides.

Several weeks earlier, Bruce had mentioned how he had a young friend who had contacted him for legal advice. He was of Indian ancestry. Freddie had recently moved from Oklahoma and had found a small house in a quiet neighborhood and had begun taking the steps necessary to purchase. Freddie was married and they had a little two- year-old daughter.

Bruce told us that Freddie was full-blooded Choctaw and his wife was Cherokee. Appleton had no problems with the Longfellow's having moved there. The problem was with the county. The property in question that they intended to buy had a big pond on it.

At some point in time the county annexed part of Appleton. Part of the proposed parcel of land the Longfellow's were trying to purchase was no longer viable as part of the sale. Freddie and family had already put a huge down payment toward that purchase. They needed help in deciding the right course of action to take. Many phone calls were made, and meetings were held with no real solution to the problem. Things got to the point where doors that were open began to close. They were going to have to accept less land and lose money or back out of the deal and still lose money.

The case had been scheduled with the Honorable Judge Amos Moses III presiding. The judge was known for his laid- back approach and fair dealings where the family was concerned. The only problem here was that he was a by-the-book sort where the law itself was concerned.

I was fortunate to be present that first day and many others as well. The bailiff introduced the judge. As he entered the courtroom, everyone noticed he had a limp. "Good morning all and please be seated. I know I will. Stepped in a darn fool hole while fishin' this weekend. Only caught one catfish and two crappy and believe me that was crappy indeed!" The whole courtroom burst out in laughter. To regain composure, he said "Now, now let us come to order. We have a serious matter to discuss. Will the lawyer representing Mr. Longfellow, I believe that would be Mr. Lightfoot, please present your case with the opening remarks?"

At that introduction, Bruce stood and began to present the case. "Your Honor and Jury members, we are here today to defend the rights and to uphold what I would call an unfair interpretation of the law. Mr. Longfellow and family moved here recently with the hope of settling into our community and becoming a productive part of our society. They located a good piece of land just to our north that promised to provide many of the things people of Indian ancestry find important. The realty agent presented the property which included a three-bedroom house with two baths, covering 1750 square feet. The house sat on 2.5 acres of land according to the information provided by the agent.

He explained, "If you choose to proceed with the sale, there has to be a good faith down payment made of $1500.00" which they agreed upon and followed through with. Two weeks later, Mr. Longfellow was contacted by the realty company and was informed that the county had informed them that the deal could not move forward as presented since there was a dispute involving the property. No further explanation had been given at that time. "My client had to call the county himself and go down to the county office to try and meet with someone to get a proper explanation", Bruce explained.

"Your Honor, Mr. Longfellow was referred back to the realty company without an explanation that he could understand. We seek a settlement of some kind that either settles this dispute or totally refunds his down payment and awards him and his family a monetary amount for the time wasted in this process."

After Bruce's opening statement, the judge then said, "Will Mr. Davidson, who I believe is representing the county please present the issues at this time?" As Bruce took his seat, he could feel the sweat running down his back, but he knew he had done his best, so far.

Ken-eth stood and began his opening statement. "If it may please the court, your Honor and members of the jury. We are here today to clear up what is simply miscommunication between parties. It is an unfortunate situation for the Longfellow family to begin with. We want to make it clear to the court that when Mr. Longfellow met with the county, they presented him with a legal explanation for the obvious misunderstanding. We hope to present testimony that will clear up the miscommunication."

Judge Moses then addressed the jury himself and gave them the duty of listening to only the information presented, so as to make the proper decision.

The trial lasted two days. The testimony given on behalf of the county was a recording of the conversation when Mr. Longfellow met with the county. That conversation was not entirely clear and included a lot of legal mumble jumble that really did not address the issue.

When the judge announced his decision, it went like this. "Mr. Longfellow, will you please stand while I read the jury's findings and by-the-way… You got a boat?" At that remark everyone went Oh-ah! And many began to clap. The judge's gavel sounded as he read "The jury has sided with The Longfellow family. They have been granted the deal originally promised with one exception. They will have to pay court costs for the county, but no further monetary obligation will be theirs from the county toward this purchase."

As soon as the decision was announced, Ken-eth glanced over at Bruce and the Longfellow's and gave them a thumbs up. As for this legal dilemma, all was well. In the months to come, there was a rumor that someone that looked kind-of-like Judge Amos Moses III was spotted fishin' with Freddie Longfellow!

CHAPTER 29
TALK ABOUT TIME

The words of the song "Time in a Bottle" say 'If I could save time in a bottle, the first thing that I'd like to do is save every day 'til eternity passes away just to spend them with you.' How profound a statement. Once again, I am sitting here typing my thoughts and memories wishing I could bottle up many of them so they would last forever.

Whether it is new beginnings or fishing with friends on a warm day, it is all about time. Perhaps, it is church on a Sunday or kids being kids, it's all about time.

Maybe, it is stepping out of your comfort zone and helping an elderly friend, it's still all about time. Life is an adventure. It has its difficulties and still more opportunities to go fishing, it's all about time. Object lessons, getting to meet girls/boys and keeping the facts straight. It's all about time.

A friendship would not be one without time being invested. "Ring, Ring, Ring" goes my phone. "Hello" is the response. "If I could make days last forever…" what would I do? Would you save every day as if they were treasures? Even when we find time, how do we spend it? Time is like the wind. It comes and it goes.

The saga of Johnny's World is about people knowing people. Young and Old, smart, and not so. It is about the tic toc of a clock. Everyone's world they live in is like Johnny's World. You have a cast of characters. You have a place to live, love and grow together. You build relationships.

I recall a sermon preached by our former Pastor Jimmy Johnson. We were young and impressionable. It was about spending time with others you care about. It dug deeper into motives behind the time we spend. Pastor Jimmy told us, "Talk comes cheap. You can say almost anything. What lies behind a spoken word is what matters. Words have an empty ring if they do not come from the heart. Without love to back up those words, nothing is truly accomplished."

He went on to say, "The Bible mentions in The Gospel of John that we must love each other as Christ loved us. Why? That our Joy may be full. Greater love has no one, than to lay down his life for a friend. What should be our motivation? In 1 Corinthians 13 we find faith, hope and love… the greatest of these is Love. Without love, God's kind of love, you are nothing but a clanging cymbal. Remember, love is surrendering to His will for YOU. You want to be someone important? Let God fill that place in your heart, so talk is not just talk and time is not just time. It is life! Letting others see Jesus in you!" Those words will forever be remembered as far as I am concerned.

Whether it be *Johnny's World,* Your World or Our World, it does not really matter. Relationships are most important wherever you are. Things happen. They are just that. Life is molded. You must work at it. Forgiveness does not exist without sacrifice. One thing to remember, is that God's forgiveness has no strings attached. It is free to us. God's ultimate sacrifice was His Son.

As I sit here, Tinsley is all grown up. Nate is being responsible while sharing experiences I had in a place we know of as Appleton, U.S.A. The little world I became a part of is called *Johnny's World.* Tinsley, Bruce, Walter, Carol, and Johnny. From these five we grew to include Ann, Debra, Diane, Ken-eth. Then relationships began with others which included Bruce Mayfield, Audrey Simpson, Patricia Newberry, Todd Jenkins, and Sue Worthington.

As Nate, I am a teacher, a husband, an aspiring writer, a mentor. As Tinsley, I am that boy who dared to enter someone else's space or "World," a friend. As Tinsley Nathaniel Thomas, I am a son, a science nerd who practically worships an encyclopedia set. As ME, I am loved by a God who gave His love to me in the form of His Son. "For God so loved the World(me), that He gave His only Son, that who-so-ever believes in Him will never perish but will have everlasting life."-John 3:16

He took the time. We must do the same. Take hold of it and let time be more than something talked about. Let it become reality. Johnny Sampson did just that. Let me tell you about my friend… Johnny Christopher Sampson.

CHAPTER 30

TINSELY, HAVE YOU HEARD FROM JOHNNY?

It was a day like any other day. I had gotten out of bed, even though Audrey had to give me a shove. I shaved & showered, and I am quite sure she appreciated it. I had a brief but meaningful breakfast, *Wow! That's a hot Pop Tart.* Grabbed my thermos of coffee and was out the door… *Oh- my kiss* "Goodbye dear, love you!" My commute to the school was normal with only a short wait for a train, this time. "Good morning's" to all the normal folks and I was at my desk to prepare for another day of classes and questions about that wonderful subject "Science."

"Ring, Ring, Ring" went my cell phone. I noticed it was coming from Walter. Why would he be calling me at this time of day?

"Hello?" I said

"Walter, is something wrong?"

All he had to say was "Tinsley, have you heard from Johnny? There was a fire and a rumor of a casualty, possibly a firefighter."

It had been a day like any other day. Monica Barnes, mother of three children, had just seen her husband Jerry out the door with a "goodbye dear" and a quick smooch as he headed to work. It had already begun raining and even worst predictions for the weather in their Portland neighborhood of Louisville, Kentucky. It was June and summer storms were predicted in that area of the world.

Monica's oldest child, Mary who was eleven going on twenty came down the stairs asking "Mom, what's for breakfast?"

She was being followed by soon-to-be five-year-old Marci. "Mom, is it my birthday, yet?"

A third child, Mark, who was eight, had been somewhat ill, so was still in bed.

The family dog, Shaggs, was curled up on the bed with Mark, neither of them desiring to get up, not even a little. It was amazing that all thunder and lightning did was to make them less interested in getting up.

Meanwhile, at Fire Station 5, it looked like a day like any other until the big boom of thunder was heard, and all knew they were in for a day not likely to be forgotten.

Johnny Sampson worked extremely hard to get his fire certification and the necessary college background to allow him to move forward. After serving at his home station in Appleton, he got a call informing him of an opening. The job was in Louisville, Kentucky. Johnny had been at #5 for nearly five years after floating for about six months. Station #5 was in a business district of Louisville. I remember Johnny telling us one day, "Man, I don't care if it gets busy seven days a week or if we spend most of our time in the kitchen or playing shuffleboard with the guys. I am a bonified firefighter and I like it where I am. Yes, I miss home, but I am helping people and serving this community. Besides, the fire chief here seems interested in my Fire prevention program."

After checking on the status of her kids, Monica Barnes headed to the kitchen to get breakfast for her and the children. The thunder and lightning had gotten worse. The rain came next. Monica noticed a spark as lightning flashed coming from behind the refrigerator right below the wall clock. A container of bacon grease had been sitting on a utility cart between the fridge and stove. Monica thought she had seen Shaggs the dog under the cart eating from his bowl when lightning hit. It scared the dog that he jumped knocking over the grease container. Sparks began to travel down the wall and ignited the grease. As soon as Monica noticed the fire had begun, she grabbed her phone and called the fire department, although the fire was spreading rapidly.

The call came into the fire station at 9:35 A.M. Johnny's captain was Melvin Singleton, a 15-year veteran firefighter. The other crew members were Pete Groverton, Charlie Collazo, and Roger Smith. The crew were on their way within 2 minutes.

Captain Singleton and his crew arrived to find Mrs. Barnes and two of her three children at the front door. They were all quite upset and frantic because a third child, Mark, who was eight was upstairs in his bedroom. Johnny very quickly grabbed the mother and brought her out the front door to stay with the other two children. An elderly neighbor, Mr. Johnson had come by and offered to stay with the family outside. Captain Singleton then said, "Sampson and Smith, go in quickly and try to get that boy out of the house. Another truck has arrived to fight the fire. Groverton and Collazo go around the back with a ladder and see if you can find another way to attack the fire."

As Johnny and Roger got halfway up the stairs, the roof above them collapsed, separating the two firefighters. Johnny quickly made it to the boy's bedroom and found Mark and the family dog huddled together in a corner.

Meanwhile, the fire had spread up the wall and onto the section of roof above the boy's bedroom. Firefighter Smith had joined the other two firefighters around the back and volunteered to climb up the roof with an axe to help reach the boy and firefighter Sampson.

At the front of the house, the other two children were so concerned about Mark and Shaggs. They were quite certain that the dog was with Mark. Shortly, a call over the radio came for Captain Singleton. It was Johnny reporting, "I found Mark and the dog, but we are trapped in the room and can see the flames from inside the room."

About that time, a news crew showed up from the local CBS Affiliate. They did not want to miss an opportunity for a story, especially one involving a child.

Fireman Smith then reported "the roof over the upstairs bedroom has collapsed. I am getting a rope down to Johnny. He plans to get the boy and his dog out through the roof.

They then heard a loud noise from within the house. At least a portion of the upstairs floor had fallen in. Captain Singleton then heard Johnny report "I have gotten Mark and Shaggs out to Roger." Another loud sound could be heard with these words from Johnny Sampson. "I see you… you're my Savior, I'm coming!" Fireman Collazo said later that just before Johnny said those words, the rope broke, having been burned by the fire.

After the fire was contained, they entered and found Johnny's body unbroken and barely singed. It was certain that he had given his life for another without a moment's hesitation.

The news crew interviewed Captain Singleton and, in his words, "Firefighter Johnny Sampson along with the crew of station #5 did what we do every time someone's life is at risk. We respond. Today, Fireman Sampson gave his life for the life of a child, his family, and their dog. Johnny was a huge asset to station #5 and will be greatly missed both professionally and personally."

As soon as I got off the phone with Walter, I called Audrey

"Have you had the T.V. on yet?"

Her response was "I was watching *The Price Is Right. Why?* Has something happened?"

I told her to try and get a national news channel right away. "There was a house fire in Louisville, and I fear we have lost our dear friend Johnny."

She said she would try. In the meantime, I began calling all our friends. That was one day I can guarantee that no one got any work done. By the end of it, we most definitely had the complete story. Johnny was being Johnny, putting others first.

Ken-eth and Bruce quickly got their legal minds together after word of this tragic incident. We knew that Johnny did not have any living family left. Johnny told Bruce that he needed to get his last will and testament together. Bruce had arranged for him to get with the right people. As far as we knew, it had been done. A phone call to a legal secretary named Jane proved true. A will had been prepared and was in a safety deposit box. Along with that were pre-paid instructions for his final arrangements.

Walter and our childhood Pastor Bro. Jimmy met to work out plans with the church's present-day Pastor for the visitation/ Memorial service. In a conversation with Fire Captain Singleton in Louisville, He had arranged it so Johnny's crew would be transported by plane to Appleton and be a part of the official fire department salute to him.

One evening while at home in my study, I reflected on a recent conversation I had with Johnny.

His voice was upbeat as he said, "Hey Tin-man. You know, none of these guys up here at the station have ever been fishin.' Can you believe that?"

"Really, Johnny. I thought you told me a while back that one of them had a boat and lived near a lake", I had replied.

"Yeah, that is Roger Smith, but he said that his brother-in-law always borrowed it, so it was hardly ever at his house. Remember that lesson we had in Sunday School about Jesus and His disciples fishin'? I bet it would be neat to get to go fishin' with Jesus. One day I will get to ask him about that, and I can go with him. Of course, we may be too busy worshipping our Lord to go fishin'", was Johnny's desire.

I could just imagine Him standing in front of our Lord and the first thing out of His mouth is "Hey, Jesus-man you want to go catch a big one?"

Jesus' reply would probably be Johnny, you already have… you have hauled in a net full and I love you for it!"

The weather was warm and sunny on the day of Johnny's memorial service. It was June 8th of that year. There were bells ringing at the near-by Catholic Church in honor of Johnny. It appeared the entire town had turned out. There were six pallbearers carrying the casket, and they were not firefighters. They were Bruce Lightfoot, Walter Davidson, Ken-eth Davidson, Todd Jenkins, Bruce Mayfield, and me. The firefighters from Louisville and those from our local fire-station were honorary pallbearers. They provided an honor guard at the cemetery.

The First Central Baptist Church of Appleton was full to the brim. Flowers galore lined the alter area up front with the casket right in the middle. It was open. Johnny had his full firefighters dress uniform and was at rest. We, who truly knew him, understood where he was. Johnny was not putting out fires. He was home in the arms of Jesus.

Walter was first up to speak after a beautiful instrumental version of Amazing Grace.

"Today is a day none of us would have wanted to come. Johnny Christopher Sampson was born here in Appleton on January 3, 1956, and went to be with the Lord on June 4, 1987. I have only a couple of things to share this morning, to the surprise of many of you. The word FAITH to many means Forsaking All I Trust Him. In Matthew 10:38-39 the Bible says, "He who is not willing to take up his cross and follow Me is not worthy of Me. He who finds his life will lose it. He who loses his life for my sake will find it. In Proverbs 3:5-6 we find "Trust in the Lord with all your heart and lean not on your own understanding, in all your ways acknowledge Him and He will direct your paths." At that, Walter took a seat.

Our former Pastor, the Rev. Jimmy Jack Johnson then came to share final words in honor and in memory of Johnny. "Thank you all for allowing me and my wife to return to Appleton to celebrate the life, not mourn the death of Johnny Sampson. He was admired by many people. You must remember though, that he was once a child and then a youth and was quite normal in all respects. All his friends looked up to him to the degree that their world was known as *Johnny's World.* Yes, you guys, I was aware of that! A key factor to that reality was his love for you all. He could do that because in John 14:15 it says, 'If you love me, keep My commandments' and that he did, most of the time. A chuckle was heard, at that comment. In Romans 10:17 it says, "Faith comes by hearing and hearing by the Word of God" His faith was indeed a strong one and in Romans 12:1-2 like most of us we try hard to "present our bodies as a living sacrifice holy, acceptable to God which is our reasonable service and be not conformed to this world but be transformed by the renewing of your mind, that you may PROVE what is that good and acceptable and perfect will of God."

The Pastor concluded, "Johnny managed to prove just that with every breath he took, ever since he asked the Lord into his life and up to that fateful day when while fighting to save others, he took his last breath and was immediately welcomed into the precious arms of Jesus."

As soon as he finished, three children came forward and sang "Jesus Loves Me." The children were not just any children, they were Marci, Mark, and Mary

Barnes, the children from the Louisville fire. Mom and Dad were on the front row so thankful to see their children paying tribute to a man who trusted a strong and mighty God.

What a time it was, all the way to the cemetery and back to the church for the customary meal. In the words of our friend Walter, "Wow! I wonder if they will have that Bird of Prey? You know Johnny would have enjoyed it!"

As I, Nate Thomas sit here sharing from my heart MY memories of *Johnny's World,* I can truly say, "Thanks for the memories, Johnny Sampson."

CHAPTER 31

THE FINAL CHAPTER: Friends never say goodbye!

Each of us, who felt to be a part of *Johnny's World,* took the day after the memorial service to meditate and allow all we had experienced to sink in a bit. I admit that it was a fact that we had just lost a very important person and puzzle piece of our life. We would never see him or hear that voice of his again. One thing for me was that I would *forever hear* him say, "Hey, Tin-Man" and nothing could remove that.

A couple of days later, we were still at Mom and Dad's. I decided to try and take my old bike out for a spin. It was still in good enough condition for riding as long as I didn't race or pop a wheelie. I wanted to do some reminiscing.

Once again, down past our block was the corner store, but the name had been changed to Nguyen's Quick Stop, and I am quite sure it wasn't any quicker.

As I came to the next street, to my surprise, there was the old Miller house, still painted in almost every color imaginable.

In the next block came a sudden rush of emotions and memories galore. It was our hometown fire station #5, with those fire trucks that were as shiny and new looking as the first day when I rode by. What especially touched my heart was a plaque hanging near that #5. It said:

In memory of our most courageous firefighter, Johnny Christopher Sampson,
Who gave his life while saving others. Sister station #5, Louisville, Kentucky
- June 4, 1987.

I immediately did as I had done many times before. I turned around to head home, only to see two familiar friends, Bruce and Walter, walking along the sidewalk. Again, I did like many times before. I honked my horn, and instead of that loud high- pitched sound, it was more like Walter's bird-of-prey.

Bruce remarked, "Hey, man, did you steal Walter's bird's voice?" At that comment we all laughed.

It seemed like yesterday, we the gang of Johnny's World… were just beginning our adventures together, and much like that last time as I took a moment to reflect.

That afternoon was spent remembering and laughing about those good times us four, and of course, the rest of our group of friends, had. We all had to get back to our everyday lives, so we said our goodbyes and went our separate ways, for now.

The drive back home didn't take but an hour and a half.

Yes, a few years ago, I had received an opportunity to go teach at a small university in our region of the state, about ninety miles from Appleton. It would mean moving from friends and family. Mom was still living in Appleton. She had retired from teaching. One day prior to making our final decision on the job offer, I went by for a visit.

"Okay, Tinsley Nathaniel… what's bothering you?" I knew she realized a serious matter was about to be discussed. After I shared some details, she explained as only she could, "Tinsley, as I have said many times before, pray for direction and follow your heart. You won't go wrong when you trust in the Lord!" Next up, I knew that I had to follow prayer with a phone call to Johnny.

I was aware that it was a scheduled day off for Johnny, so when the phone rang about six times, I got concerned.

"Yello," Johnny answered. "Sampson's answering service!"

"Johnny, it's me, Tinsley Nathaniel," I said in a somewhat frantic voice.

"Oh, hey, Tin-Man! What's up?"

Seriously, I asked, "Where were you? The phone rang forever, and I got concerned."

"You knew this was a day off for me. I was outside at a neighbor's house. They have a boy named Joe who is ten years old. His dad is in the military overseas. I was playing catch with him and his football. He is a good kid, and I thought he might need a friend. I know I am not his dad, but I can be that friend."

For a moment, I forgot why I called.

I did eventually get to the reason I had called, and he did support my decision to take the position at the school, but I was amazed at what a devoted friend he could be.

It was weeks after the funeral service; I was going through some stuff in our garage. I was looking in a storage bin from years back. It was identified as *High School Years*. I brought the bin inside the house and sat it on the dining table. Audrey was in a nearby room, so she came in and asked, "What's going on? Tinsley, what all is in that container?"

I explained, "It has a bunch of things from our high school days. I was curious, so I brought it in to see what memories I might find."

Audrey remarked, "Maybe you should fear some of it, you never know…out of sight, out of mind."

"I had forgotten that Johnny had been notorious for having someone taking quick snapshots when you weren't expecting it." As soon as those words came out of my mouth, I saw pictures from the day of our football tryouts. There were pictures of Audrey and Patricia Newberry and their girlfriends in the stands and on the sidelines. Then, I found a picture of when Johnny had thrown that pass to me right when Audrey had yelled, "Go Nate!" Bloody nose and bruised face. Also, a picture of Walter when he first saw the bird-of-prey. Walter's eyes were wide opened with that look… come to think of it, quite normal for Walter.

While looking through the bin, I came upon a group picture that I had taken that included Johnny's sister Ann and her eventual husband Bruce. It was rare to have a picture of Bruce, and come to think of it, we never really got to see Ann long enough for any picture taking. I recall that on the day of his service, Ann and Bruce had to leave right after the funeral. Audrey told me, "Ann thanked us all for helping with the planning and everything else, but they had to get back to the store. It appeared that they didn't feel comfortable around the family." I had wished that things could have gone differently between Ann and her parents.

Johnny mentioned one day, "My mom and dad keeps riding Ann so much about her spending too much time around that Mayfield boy." They kept saying that nothing good would come out of it. The real problem was that Johnny knew he was in a difficult situation, straining their relationship.

"T-Man, my parents don't seem to recognize true love and how it effects young folk, and I honestly believe that Ann and Bruce's love is truly genuine."

One thing about Johnny that everyone would agree with was that he kept his word and always seemed to have an eye on the future. I remember those words he said to me on the day we moved into Appleton.

With his hand of friendship and those words "Can I help? He genuinely meant "Welcome to our life; you're now a part of it!"

From that very first day and every day after, Johnny Sampson had made sure this nerdy boy from the east was included. I recall when I told him, "Johnny, I don't think they like me", referencing the neighborhood kids on that day.

"Oh, give them time, they'll come around," he assured me.

As I continued to look through the bin of memories, I saw this purple envelope with rainbows on it. It appeared to have never been opened. As Audrey looked over my shoulder, I gave her a quick glance of wonderment because it was addressed to our friend Carol and had Johnny's return address, but no stamp. "Audrey, I'm going to open it!"

Inside this colorful envelope was a birthday card with a letter in it. The card was a "Happy 21st Birthday" card. As I recalled, both Carol and Walter were born in February of the same year. Carol was thirteen days older than Walter. After Walter and Carol had started "dating", he would often refer to himself as a "love child', since he was actually born on Valentines Day, therefore, he was destined for L-O-V-E.

As I began to open the letter, I looked at Audrey and said, "Should I be doing this? I could just give the card and letter to Carol. After all, it is addressed to her."

Audrey quickly responded, "Nate, it was not mailed for some reason. Let's read it and see if we can figure out why." I opened the letter and began to read.

Dear Carol,

On this your 21st birthday, I feel the need to tell you how wonderful a person you are and to apologize for the way we "friends" have treated you from time to time. You have been a great across-the -street neighbor forever, it seems, and I sometimes wonder if Walter has noticed you as he should. He appears to spend more time joking around and treating you as the punchline, as if he would even have to. It is very noticeable to me how you feel about him. You need to step it up and tell him the way it is. If you don't, who knows what he may do. Enough said. I hope you enjoy your birthday.

Your friend and

matchmaker, Johnny

Sampson.

"Oh, my!", I said. "Audrey, if this letter had been mailed and Walter had found out, things might not have turned out as they did. I am so glad Johnny changed his mind, but why didn't he destroy it?"

After giving it some thought, I said, "I recall us four guys, Johnny, Walter, Bruce and myself, sitting around in our backyard around that time, talking about girls, dating and future plans, when suddenly Walter shocked us with "Oh, I almost forgot. Carol and I are getting married.""

"When is this happening, and does Carol know?" I asked.

Now I understood. "Audrey, I remember that almost as soon as Walter shared that information, Johnny had jumped up suddenly and asked to be excused… something about needing to check his mail. He must have put it out to be picked up by the mail carrier, but you know, there was no stamp on it."

Upon further examination of the envelope, we could see that the stamp had been removed. As I put the card back in the envelope, I noticed that there was something else inside. It was a note that said,

Tin-Man,

This just goes to show you that even I can misjudge and ALMOST goof up a good thing. Thank the Lord for His will and interference or should I say, Guidance.

Your eternal

friend, Johnny.

All I could do after reading that was to smile and give my wife the biggest hug possible.

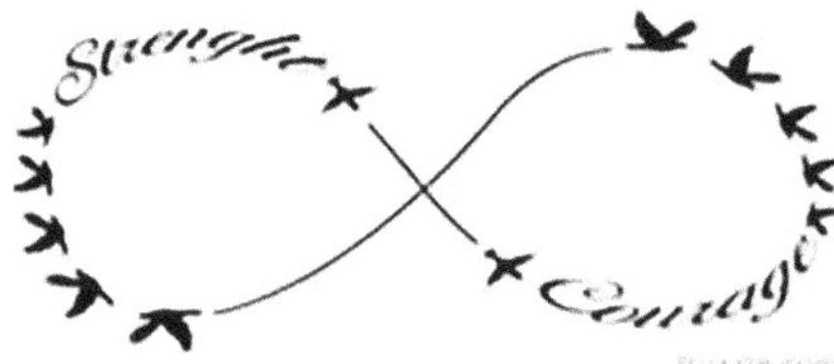

The anticipation of a phone call can be pleasant when you expect it and have an idea what it will be about, but not at all when it may never happen again. It makes you regret the times you got that call and wished you hadn't answered. Good times produce good calls. Challenging times bring frustration and unrest. One such call had come about a year before Johnny's passing. The phone rang late one night, sometime before midnight. I had been doing some late-night typing and was preparing for bed. I allowed it to ring about three or four times, hoping that it might be a wrong number. I reluctantly answered, "Hello, Thomas residence?"

It was Johnny calling from Louisville. "Tin-man, this is Johnny. I am sorry to be calling so late. It is actually an hour later here. I just had to talk to someone. We responded to a fire earlier today that got pretty rough. It was an apartment fire that affected adjoining apartments. It had begun upfront and had spread very quickly toward the rear of the complex."

"The problem with these back apartments", he continued, "Was that they had a wooden fence behind them, which made it more difficult to gain access to them without going all the way to the street and back around, so it forced us to call another unit to assist with the fire. This delayed our assessment of the rear apartment."

He went on to explain the worst of the ordeal. "By the time we had contact with anyone back there, the apartment was fully engaged. A family of five, which included a grandmother who had been bed/wheelchair bound for some time. The parents were able to get their two children out safely. The father went back in to try to rescue his mom but could not get through the inferno. He got second and third degree burns on his arms, hands, and face. "Johnny seemed to choke up a bit but continued. "The grandmother was pronounced dead at the scene." As he fought back the tears, he said, "Man, this one hit me hard. You know I spent a lot of time studying and researching fire prevention and about fire codes. This fire didn't have to end with this result."

This was one of those times when I felt so inadequate. What could I say or suggest that would help at this time of need? The only thing I could do was recite scripture that our pastors had shared in time of need. One such passage was found in 1 John 4.

"Johnny, the most important thing anyone can do is to make sure your main purpose for your actions is love. The Holy Spirit wants to help us share God's love in what we say and do. 'Herein is our love made perfect, that we may have boldness… there is no fear in love… we love Him because He first loved us, so we must show that love.' You are doing that every time you go on a run. Just make sure your heart is filled with that love and that your intentions are pure. Johnny, I have no doubt about your intentions. Trust in God, and He will give you strength!"

After that conversation, he didn't miss any opportunity to do or thank me for encouraging him.

Once again, I found myself sitting at my desk, attempting to do some sort of creative writing that would be worthy to share with my students, when I suddenly recalled words spoken by my poetic friend Johnny Sampson: "When words fail to come, and you just can't find them, perhaps the answer isn't found from poets or theologians. Why not go grab that pole and go to the hole and let that fish do the biting?" At that thought of wisdom, I arose from my desk and headed out the door, fishing gear in hand… and a whistle to step to!

Yes, life in *Johnny's World* was much like a day of fishin'. Johnny often say, "If you want to catch that big one, be patient; it will come to you as sure as the weather changes." As I look back with fond memories, I know, *all is right in Johnny's World!*"

AUTHOR'S BIOGRAPHY

JOHN W. SANGWIN

The author of Johnny's World: The Series-in-one is J.W. Sangwin. This is a collaboration of five smaller published books with some minor editing in the hope that this book will give you a much clearer and more enjoyable picture. John is married to Patricia Tisdale Sangwin, and they reside in Port Arthur, Texas. John is also the published author of A Storybook Collection. Please share this book with others and always look on the positive side of life. Just remember: Jesus really cares about you!